I0547121

Rich in Faith

Lindi Peterson

Copyright © 2015 Lindi Peterson

This is a work of fiction. Names, characters, places and incidents are either the products of the authors imagination or are used fictitiously. Any resemblance to actual persons (living or dead), events or locations is entirely coincidental.

Printed and bound in the United States of America.

All rights reserved. No part of this book may be reproduced in any form or by any electronic or mechanical means, including information storage and retrieval systems, without permission in writing from the author, except by a reviewer who may quote brief passages in a review.

ISBN: 978-1-942419-01-3

Cover design: Lynnette Bonner
indiecoverdesign@blogspot.com
Cover images © Dreamstime.com: 9759459 10225327 8542973
Editor: Emily Sewell

DEDICATION

To my husband Lenny.
I love you.

Other Novels by Lindi Peterson

Her Best Catch

Summer's Song

Richness in Faith Trilogy
Rich in Love
Rich in Hope

Coming Soon
The Wedding Dress Collection Series
The Little Black Wedding Dress—Summer 2015
The Bride Wore Red----Fall 2015

www.lindipeterson.com

"And why do you worry about clothes?

See how the lilies of the field grow. They do not labor or spin."

Matthew 6:28 NKJV

MISTAKE

AS I STAND on Peachtree Street in downtown Atlanta waiting for a cab to take me to the airport, I'm reminded of the night I lost my faith. At least that's what Mama would have called my lapse in judgment.

Losing my faith.

A muggy haze hangs over the evening, reminiscent of that long-ago night. Paul Wenthworth had been my boyfriend for awhile. He was also the richest guy in school, so when I envisioned our first time together, I thought it would happen in a grand place, like his parents' weekend lake house.

Or maybe an elegant hotel, like the Ritz at Lenox.

So imagine my disappointment when he pulled up to a motel on the outskirts of nowhere important.

More than ten years have passed, but it seems like nothing has changed.

My wealthy, attractive fiancé has dumped me for the heiress of a clothing company, claiming he's finally found true love. Simply a coincidence that his break up came shortly after dinner at my parents' house.

Trailer.

House trailer.

So I, Shelby Madison, am left on the outskirts of nowhere important once again.

Alone.

Alone and more determined than ever not to let anyone in. It's too hard when they tell you they want out.

"WHAT DO YOU mean the position is filled? There must be a mistake. Barb Simmons said she had arranged everything." Unable to calm my racing heart, I stand in the foyer of the Hampton Cove mansion, my two suitcases flanking either side of me. My backpack straps cut into my shoulder while my overly large purse is about to break my forearm.

"I believe Ms. Simmons was misinformed regarding the position of housekeeper." The older, sturdy woman isn't mean. No, adamant is more like it. "I'm the housekeeper. And I intend to keep my position."

My purse slips off my forearm and plummets to the rug. "Ms...?"

"*Mrs.* Stratton."

"*Mrs.* Stratton. Are you sure there hasn't been a mistake? Do you know Barb? Why would she let me sublet my Atlanta apartment for the summer if you had no intention of leaving your job?"

Mrs. Stratton shoves her hands inside the pockets of her gray, knee-length uniform. "The name Simmons sounds familiar. I believe Mr. and Mrs. Simmons are friends of Mr. Treyhune. But I haven't any idea why she would arrange for your trip here. Why don't you call and ask her?"

The events of the last couple of weeks have really worn on my brain. Of course I need to call Barb. "I will."

Before I can rummage through my purse which still sits on the rug, a scream fills the air. Startled, I look at Mrs. Stratton who simply rolls her eyes.

Then two flashes of small bodies with very long black hair rush across what appears to be a formal living room.

Another girl, this one in her twenties, enters the living room from the same direction the small girls did. But she doesn't follow their path. No, she walks towards Mrs. Stratton and me.

She has a purse slung over her shoulder and a frown on her face. She holds a key out toward Mrs. Stratton. "Here. Tell Mr. Treyhune I'm done. I can't work out my notice. It's not worth the money. That's how done I am."

Mrs. Stratton doesn't say anything, but she does take the key.

The girl who couldn't work her notice stares at me momentarily before taking in my luggage. She shakes her head. "If you're the new nanny, good luck is all I can say."

With those words, she passes by me, her sweet smelling perfume moving along with her.

After the door clicks shut I look at Mrs. Stratton. "The new nanny?"

She shakes her head. "The previous nanny left almost a month ago. Tracy was filling in until Mr. Treyhune could hire someone else. Maybe Mrs. Simmons arranged *that* position for you."

I shudder. "I doubt it. I don't have any experience taking care of a child, let alone two."

"And they're a pair, all right."

As if they'd been summoned the girls fly back across the living room in the direction from which they had come a couple of minutes ago. They are still screaming.

Covering my ears, I kind of hunch down. "Does that go on a lot?"

"Depends."

"On what?"

"On lots of things. If you want to stay, I'll show you your room."

I uncover my ears then run my hand through my hair. "No. I don't want to stay. Can I talk to Mr. Treyhune?"

Mrs. Stratton chuckles. "You may. You can pull up a couch until he arrives home from work about nine o'clock this evening."

"Nine? That's late." Memories of my long days as CFO at Brady Engineering fill my mind. There were times I considered leaving at nine o'clock leaving early. Of course a lot of those times I was working closely with Dale. Dale Brady had started the company, hired me as the CFO and together we had built a nice business.

And a nice relationship. The fourth finger on my left hand is now void of the engagement ring he gave me.

Then took back.

I wonder if he'll give his new girlfriend a ring someday and if so, will it be the same ring?

I need a distraction from these thoughts that keep assailing me. Will Dale ever leave my brain? "I could go to Mr. Treyhune's office if you give me the address."

"He has several offices. One at each dealership. Treyhune Chevrolet, Treyhune Ford, Treyhune Dodge. Take your pick. Maybe you'll get lucky."

I steady my hand on my luggage handle. "Mr. Treyhune is *that* Treyhune?"

Mrs. Stratton looks at me like I've grown two heads. "What do you mean by *that* Treyhune?"

"Please don't tell me he's the racing Treyhune. The one that won all the championships way back."

She shakes her head. "He's not that Treyhune."

My nerves steady. "Okay. Good."

"He's his son. Court."

I stand stunned. My dad would have a heart attack if he had an inkling his daughter was standing in the home of Court Treyhune. The fact that he couldn't ever live up to his father's racing greatness made him no less important in the eyes of the racing fans.

They still loved him.

According to the media what Court lacked in driving ability, he made up for in his looks and charitable doings. Great. "Court Treyhune. And these are his daughters?"

"They are. Bristol and Darling."

I laugh at the irony. "Race tracks." I point to myself. "I'm named after a car, myself. Shelby. Shelby Madison."

Mrs. Stratton cracks a smile for the first time in our conversation. "Nice to meet you, Shelby."

"His wife died a couple of years ago, didn't she?"

"Yes. I only knew her a short time before she passed away. I started working here when they moved in, but she didn't live long after the move. She was very sick."

I'm not telling Mrs. Stratton I feel like I know the Treyhunes. My dad is a huge fan, and I probably know way more about them than any sane person should. And half the stuff my dad told me, I tuned out. Like maybe the fact that Court Treyhune lived in Hampton Cove, Florida. "I'm sorry to hear that. I'm sure the girls miss their mother."

"They do. And now it looks like I'm not only the housekeeper but the nanny for the rest of the day."

I rummage through my purse and find my phone. Two o'clock. I could go and try to catch Court Treyhune at one of his offices. Or I could stay here until he comes home.

I hold my phone up. "I'm going to call my friend Barb and see what is going on."

"That sounds like a good idea." Mrs. Stratton's expression matches my thoughts.

I turn away as my phone connects to Barb's and starts ringing. It rings several times and when it connects to her voicemail, I leave a message for her to call me back. As soon as I hang up, the two girls, whose screams had been silent for the last few minutes, come flying from the right once again. But this time they head straight for Mrs. Stratton.

Mrs. Stratton who almost falls as each girl grabs onto one leg. I reach out and steady the older lady. I notice the girls' faces are tear-streaked and they are identical. They're both sobbing, then one of them starts hitting the other one on the arm.

"Stop hitting me." The girl being hit pushes off Mrs. Stratton and plops on the floor.

"You stop pulling my hair. Tracy left because of you." The other girl makes no move, continuing to cling tightly to the housekeeper.

The housekeeper who was obviously right about being the nanny for the rest of the day.

"She did not," the other girl counters. "She left 'cause you have a big mouth and won't be quiet."

I wonder which one is Darling. Although it really doesn't matter. They both seem "too tough to tame," the nickname for Darlington Motor Speedway.

And racing at Bristol Motor Speedway is like driving around inside a fishbowl, cars always wrecking. Are their names premonitions of their lives?

Crazy.

I know too much about a sport I dislike.

Silence hovers, and in looking down at the crumpled girls, I decide they've run out of steam. At least for a minute.

Maybe Mrs. Stratton will have a reprieve.

My phone vibrates and I see that it is Barb calling. I answer quickly.

"Barb. It's Shelby, hi. I'm at the Treyhune home, but there's some sort of mistake. I'm standing here with Mrs. Stratton. The housekeeper. Who has no intention of leaving her job. So, I'm confused as to why I'm here."

"Shell, sweets. So glad you made it. While I've got you on the phone I must tell you Rhea, the gal who sublet your place, loves it. She's thrilled with it. Okay, I'm at my desk, I know the information is here somewhere, bear with me a moment, sweets."

I can hear ruffling and shuffling going on as my body relaxes knowing that momentarily this mix-up will be solved. "I'm bearing."

"Ah. Here it is. I wrote it all down while I was talking to Court. Such a precious man. Single, too."

"Barb, please. I need a distraction from the male population."

"He'll distract you, all right. Sweets, here's all the info. Nanny needed for the summer. Gal gave two-weeks notice. Come as soon as you can."

My relief swiftly tenses. "Barb. You told me housekeeper." I lower my voice to whisper status and move as far away from Mrs. Stratton and the twins as possible. "Remember? I needed to get away and do something totally different for a couple of months. Cleaning houses I can do. It's in my blood. Kids? No."

"Housekeeper, nanny. All the same. Domestic help, right?"

I'm surprised the phone doesn't shatter in my hand at the tight grip I have on it. "No, Barb. Not the same at all."

"Shells. You're a whiz at whatever you do. And you wanted a change of pace. I'm sure you can handle any position Court has for you. Need to run. Love."

"Love." My tone is flat as the phone is now silent.

I drop my phone in my purse and slowly turn. Mrs. Stratton is staring at me.

So are the two girls.

"Are you our new nanny?" The one who asks scoots closer to the other girl, like they are a team and a force to be reckoned with.

Even at their young age they know this.

I don't know if I am the one who can reckon with Team Twin.

But it appears I'm the one hired to do just that.

BRISTOL AND DARLING stick close to me as I unpack my suitcases in my room, which is directly across from the media room and the girls' bedrooms. They each have their own room but sleep in the same bed. Mrs. Stratton, who, even though I told her to call me Shelby didn't offer to let me call her anything but Mrs. Stratton, told me the girls have never slept in separate rooms.

It doesn't escape my notice that our quarters are on one side of the mansion while Court's quarters are on the other side.

Mrs. Stratton is allowed to leave after dinner.

Lucky lady.

"Did you bring any fun clothes?"

As I can't tell the twins apart, I'm not sure which one asks me the question. "What do you mean by fun clothes?"

She picks up a blouse that I had laid on the bed. "This is for when you go to work. What about shorts? T-shirts?"

Considering I'd spent the last five years working, I probably don't have many fun clothes. Then the night I packed, shortly after being dumped by Dale, I basically shoved what I could into the suitcases, not thinking about having any kind of fun.

Especially considering I was in a funk of the worst kind.

Still am if I'm honest.

You don't get over a serious relationship in a minute.

Dale's face appears in front of my eyelids every time I shut them. His betrayal has consumed me, and I stupidly thought putting literal distance between us would help.

But every item of clothing reminds me of times spent with him.

"This is ugly."

I knowingly narrow my eyes at the child.

She narrows her eyes back at me.

I'm frustrated that I don't know which half of Team Twin I'm narrowing my eyes at.

Sighing, I dig through my make-up bag. Spying a smaller plastic bag, I pull it out and open it.

I look at the girl who told me my shirt was ugly. "Which one are you?"

"Bristol." Her tone is defiant, while her face looks angelic.

"Hold out your hand."

She continues to stare.

"Now."

"Please?" Her tone is mimicking. I wonder who she's mimicking.

"Please hold out your hand." Oh, I'm not cut out for this job. Give me some financial plans to assess. Some figures to analyze.

Bristol holds out her hand, and I slip a black elastic pony-tail holder around her wrist.

I look at Darling. "Your turn. Please."

Darling copies her twin, and I slip a red one on her.

"I want you to leave these on your wrists until I can learn to tell you apart. Deal?"

They look at each other and smile. "Cool. These are Granddaddy's racing colors." Bristol looks at me. "Did you know that?"

Cal Treyhune's colors. Black and red. "Maybe."

Subconsciously I'm sure I did.

I lay the bag of elastic bands on the bed. The two girls could put those bands to use with their thick black hair. I can't imagine brushing through what looks like lots of tangles, but keeping it in a ponytail will be a huge help in taming it.

I'll tackle their hair as soon as I've put my clothes away.

"Bristol. Do you know telling people their clothes are ugly is rude?"

She plays with the band on her wrist. "I'm just being honest."

"Sometimes you need to keep your honesty to yourself. You can hurt people's feelings."

"Did I hurt your feelings?"

To tell the child I have no feelings because they'd been trampled upon, stomped out, and ground into the cement sidewalk seems dramatic. I simply say, "No. But it's not polite."

Neither is telling your friend there's a housekeeping job open when it's really a nanny job, but I can't be too mad at Barb. She's a great friend, and I know in her heart, she was doing what she thought I wanted.

And I suppose if I have to hang somewhere for three months, this mansion isn't the worst place I could have landed.

"Ow!"

My attention focuses back on the twins where it appears Bristol has popped Darling's elastic band. A red ring shows up against Darling's wrist.

"Bristol. Apologize to your sister."

She pops the elastic band again before folding her arms over her chest. She then looks at me with a rebellious stare. I've dealt with a lot of people in my life, but they've all been over four feet tall and had more than a few years on them.

Dealing with this little set of dynamite twins has me in a place I've never been before.

I never saw this coming.

Not at all.

I reach out and pop Bristol's band.

"Hey, ow. What'd you do that for?"

"I wanted to show you how it feels. It doesn't feel good, does it?"

She continues to rub her wrist. "I didn't pop Darling's that hard. I'm gonna tell my dad tonight. He'll fire you."

"Fine by me. Why don't you two go play while I finish hanging up my clothes. This must be boring for you. I'll be done shortly."

Bristol sits on the floor, and Darling follows.

"Okay." I drape a long-sleeved black shirt on a hanger. "If you want to be bored, you are allowed."

The next few minutes is spent unpacking. Every now and then I glance at the girls, and I notice they watch with interest as I deal with my wardrobe.

"Miss Madison?"

I jump and the twins giggle as Mrs. Stratton's voice comes over an intercom system. Bristol pops up, Darling right behind her, and they run over to the wall where the intercom box is located.

Bristol pushes a button. "Hi, Mrs. Stratton."

"Dinner is ready."

The girls run out of the room before I can digest what Mrs. Stratton has said. As I take in her words, I realize I now may have a few minutes to myself while the girls eat.

Arriving as emotionally exhausted as I did, and then dealing with the position mix-up, I'm ready for some blank space in my brain. But the space isn't blank very long before Dale's features bleed blue all over the emptiness.

Wanting nothing more than to plop on the floor like Bristol did earlier and throw a tantrum like I'm sure she's capable of, I squelch the overflow of emotions once again, and continue to unpack, my movements almost robot-like. I feel like I'm in a trance.

A hazed trance of betrayal, loss and loneliness.

Add to that secrecy (I cannot tell my father whose house I'm in) and confusion (those twins not only look alike, but their whole presence breeds confusion), and I don't know how I'm functioning.

A hot bath would be a temporary remedy. Maybe after the girls go to bed, I can indulge in bubbles.

Before I can fully explore how I might be relaxing later, Mrs. Stratton's voice blares over the intercom. "Miss Madison. We are waiting for you."

Waiting for *me*?

And who is *we*?

Instead of playing with the intercom, I walk to the kitchen. A keeping room sits adjacent to the kitchen and the back wall is nothing but glass. A sweeping view of the bay sits beyond clusters of palms. A black wrought iron fence lines the back of the property.

Mrs. Stratton walks to me. "You'll become used to that view quickly. Until then, it's dinnertime."

I doubt I'll become used to the view. Can one ever become used to such luxury and grandness?

I hadn't seen the girls in the dining room as I passed by and there is no one sitting at the bar with its beautiful granite counter top.

"What does dinnertime have to do with me?" I am hungry, but assuming I'm on my own, I wasn't going to think about dinner until later. I'm not used to eating until eight or nine most evenings.

"It's part of the job requirement to eat all meals with them."

"Even though I've unpacked, until I talk to Mr. Treyhune I don't know that I am officially hired. I imagine the man would want to approve the person who will be taking care of his children."

She chuckles. "I can safely say Mr. Treyhune will approve of you wholeheartedly. And Mr. Treyhune trusts my judgment as well. I've already spoken with him and you are, by all means, hired. Although he will run a background check. Since you've come by way of a recommendation from Mrs. Simmons, I assume you have a clean history."

"I do." Unless thoughts of murdering a cheating ex-boyfriend show up. Then, not so much.

"Follow me. The girls are waiting."

Obviously still in my robotic state, I follow Mrs. Stratton through the keeping room and out the French doors that lead to the terrace.

A beautiful, modernly sleek kitchen lines the patio. A pool, hot tub, and comfy furniture also are in view. The girls are sitting at a table, their hair blowing with the wind.

Their feet kick the air, a sign of their restlessness. I walk over to them, noticing Mrs. Stratton makes her way back through the doors into the house.

They smile as I approach.

"Yay!" Bristol claps. "We can eat."

I can't see her face for her hair blowing in front of it. "Here, give me your elastic band."

As I reach for her wrist, she pulls it back. "No."

Darling takes her elbows off the table, and places her hands in her lap, safely away from my grasp, I'm thinking.

"Why? You can't eat with that hair in your face."

"I don't like bands in my hair."

I see what I can only describe as panic in her dark eyes. They are opened wide, her gaze moving rapidly from me to her wrist.

Do I want to fight this battle? They've been eating for years without me. Maybe I should just trust this.

But by nature I want to fix it. And I'm not sure if I can sit watching them try to put food in their mouth around all that hair.

"How about this?" I scoop Bristol's hair and tuck it inside the back of her shirt.

She scrunches her shoulders and moves her head back and forth, but her hair isn't in her face.

"Is that okay?" I ask.

She quits struggling. "Sure."

I do the same for Darling before sitting down at the table.

My hair is already up in a loose bun, so I'm out of the hair issue.

Picking up my fork, the breeze pushes the aroma of the food to me. Chicken with an Alfredo-looking sauce, cut-up broccoli, pasta covered with cheese and a slice of bread cover my plate.

"Aren't you going to say grace?" Darling asks.

It's then I notice neither one of them have eaten anything.

Inwardly I groan. Daddy loves NASCAR and Mama loves Jesus. I've spent the last ten years distancing myself from both. If I never hear about another race that will be fine with me.

And as far as Jesus goes? I surprise my mother with occasional visits to her church. I'm not opposed to Jesus.

I'm just not rambunctious about Him.

"Sure." I look at Darling. "You can say grace."

The twins start the "God is great, God is good" prayer, which brings back memories of sitting in vacation Bible school at snack time.

As soon as the prayer is done they start eating. I notice they aren't eating the same meal I am. They have big, fat, juicy hotdogs and French fries on their plates.

What's up with that?

How many different meals does Mrs. Stratton cook?

I look at Bristol and Darling as they shove fries in their mouth while a few strands of their hair escape my make-shift remedy. Glancing at the beautiful surroundings, I can't help but wonder if they take this place for granted.

Their life is different from so many others.

A bay-scented breeze blows across the patio and with it comes a revelation.

I'm now living the childhood I'd always wanted.

Only I'm not the child.

I'm the nanny.

MADHOUSE

SHEER EXHAUSTION is the only way the girls finally fall asleep.

After an hour of arguing, fighting and refusing to take a bath, I made them crawl in their bed and stood by their door.

I didn't even attempt to brush their hair.

This can't continue.

Mrs. Stratton is still here. She offered to stay until Mr. Treyhune comes home.

It's ten after nine and he's not here yet.

I'm sitting at the kitchen bar, laptop open, determined to make a schedule of sorts.

I have no idea what I'm doing.

"Hello. You must be the new nanny."

Looking up I have to blink a couple of times as I'm unprepared for the magnificence of the man who must be Court Treyhune. Gulping, I remember seeing him on television from time to time years ago, decked out in his racing attire, microphone shoved in his face.

But in person, looking at Court is like being given air to breathe. Well built, his black hair and dark eyes are a perfect combination, accentuating his handsome face.

I breathe deeply once again.

"Are you all right?" he asks.

Fingers hovering above my keyboard, I nod. Sheer exhaustion has overtaken me as well.

Mrs. Stratton, who had been in the keeping room flipping through a magazine, has now walked into the kitchen.

"Good evening, Mr. Treyhune. I'd like to introduce you to Shelby Madison, your new nanny. She's the woman Mrs. Simmons recommended."

Court cocks his head in a questioning way. Like he's trying to recall a conversation. Or maybe he's trying to recall who Barb is.

"Ah, yes. Barb and Jim Simmons. From Atlanta. I'm assuming you're from Atlanta?"

I wouldn't call Court's tone slow or curious. More like cautious.

"Yes. I'm from Atlanta." That's all the information he's getting. He's not getting that I grew up in a trailer park. He's not getting that I grew up materially underprivileged but over loved. These things he would never understand.

"How long have you been a nanny?" He sets some papers on the bar countertop. His forearms look extra-strong peeping out from the rolled up dark-brown sleeves of his button-up oxford. The shirt almost matches his eyes, which are focusing on me.

Unknowingly forcing me to tell the truth. I look at my watch. "Six hours give or take."

He doesn't laugh, smile, or in any way acknowledge that I might be telling a funny story. "I'll give you a week."

I close out of the program I am working on and shut my laptop while trying to shake off the agitated feeling his statement has caused. "I wasn't informed of any type of probationary period."

Now his lips turn up slightly. "Oh, it's not a probationary period. It's how long I think you'll last before you pack your bags."

His remark raises many questions. "Do you have that little faith in me or that much faith in your daughters?"

As I hear Mrs. Stratton suck in a breath, I wonder if I'll still be employed after he speaks.

Shifting eyes and a barely there frown don't take away from his handsome factor, but they do delay his response. "I don't have any faith. In anything. Now, if you don't mind, I'd like to ask you a few questions since my girls' lives are in your hands for the next three…well for a little while, anyway."

I'm nervous about what Barb told him about me. Not that I've done anything bad, but there are certain parts of my life I like kept quiet. I've shared with Barb some of my fears, angst and other information that aren't commonly known.

I hope she didn't feel the need to relay too much to Court.

Thank goodness I didn't tell her about my NASCAR dislike. Of course there would be no good reason to talk to a downtown city gal like Barb about a racing sport.

But she is friends with Court.

"Now that you're home, Mr. Treyhune, I'll be leaving. I'll see you in the morning." Mrs. Stratton turns to me. "Good night, Shelby. I'll see you in the morning as well. Hopefully."

She says the last word so quietly, I barely hear her.

Court and I both say goodbye and Mrs. Stratton walks down the long hallway, past the girls' rooms to the garage.

"I'm going to grab a beer. Do you want one?" Court asks.

Actually, I would love a beer, but refined ladies don't sit around chugging beer. Not in my world. "No. Thanks for asking, though." Polite.

After grabbing a beer from the fridge, he digs in a drawer until he comes up with a bottle opener. After popping the top, he takes a long swig. His right hand grips the counter and he tilts the bottle toward me. "Let me guess. You're more of a Pinot Noir lady, right?"

How did he know my favorite wine I pretend to like? Did Barb tell him? Not that she knows I pretend. But certainly Barb and Court weren't that intimate in their conversation about me. Unless he asked if I was a drinker. I would want to know if the person I was hiring to take care of my children took to the bottle too much.

Although the way he is swigging that beer, I'm wondering what too much would be to him. "I've been known to drink a glass of red wine." I refuse to reveal unimportant personal information to him.

He sets the beer bottle on the counter and retrieves a bottle from the wine rack. He holds it up. "I have a 2006 Freeman Sonoma Coast."

He has no idea how his wine knowledge is being wasted on me. The 2006 Free whatever he just spouted off means nothing to me. Again, something he doesn't need to know. "Yes. I'd love a glass." I watch as he goes straight to the wine glasses, makes absolutely no production out of uncorking the wine, then pours a small amount into the glass and hands it to me, as if I am at a restaurant and he is the waiter.

Hot waiter.

I start to take a sip, then remember I'm supposed to smell it first. So I back off the sip, make a show of inhaling, then wet my pallet with the wine. Which tastes like red wine.

I hold out my glass and he pours until my glass is half full.

"Join me outside?" He sets the bottle on the counter, grabs his beer, then walks to the doors opening to the terrace.

Following him I find myself holding tightly onto the wine glass. I should probably be holding the glass by the stem. I hope my tenseness doesn't shatter the glass.

It's a good thing I'm only here for three months.

Maybe. Court doesn't think I'll last the week.

We walk outside. The breeze hits me as I shut the door. Court passes the four barstools that invite you to sit at the counter of the outdoor kitchen with the amazing pizza oven. I wonder how many times that's been used?

Maybe the girls like pizza.

As Court sits at one end of the couch, I sit as far away as possible at the other end, which isn't as far as I would like it to be. As I sip my wine, I realize I'm probably going to have to drink the whole glass. Dale's love of good wine led to him finishing up my wine if I didn't.

And I usually didn't.

I have yet to become a connoisseur of wine, but it was what people in Dale's world drank.

And I so wanted to be in Dale's world.

Even if it meant faking a love of wine.

It's dark as we sit, only the lights shining from inside the house break the night. Court seems content with the atmosphere.

He looks at me, his expression tired. "Barb Simmons talked you up on the phone. She said you were a financial whiz needing a break. She didn't tell me you were pretty, though."

Pulling my gaze away from my wine glass that is half-way to my lips, I stare at him. "Pretty?"

Raising his eyebrows, he grins. "I sense a bigger agenda on the part of Barb."

Looking into the wine, I wonder if he's put something in there to make me clueless. Discovering only burgundy-looking water, I return my attention to Court. "I don't know what you're implying."

Sitting straighter he places his elbows on his knees, the beer bottle dangling from his fingertips. "Barb sends a pretty woman down here with absolutely no experience at being a nanny. Sounds like she's matchmaking to me."

My face flushes at his insinuation. I can't even respond to his comment.

"Barb always wants everyone to be happy. That's her nature." He takes a long swallow of his beer.

If I don't speak he'll assume he's right. If I do speak will it come out sounding like I'm defending myself? I need to say something. "Barb's not matchmaking."

That was uneventful and not very convincing, I'm afraid.

"A bold statement. A bold statement from someone who's single and never been a nanny."

Taking a sip of my wine is better than telling him about Dale and what transpired over the last couple of weeks that led to me sitting in a mansion, far away from my home, hired as a nanny for a guy that my dad would love to meet.

And he thinks Barb and I orchestrated all this?

We couldn't have planned this fiasco.

Court doesn't take his gaze from me. Still, Dale's face looms before me. Our love, my whole former life with Dale, floats between Court and me.

"I prefer blondes. Barb knows that." He sets his beer bottle on the tiled terrace next to the couch. It tilts for a moment before settling, but Court doesn't notice.

He reaches into his back pocket, pulls out his wallet, and hands me a small photo. I have to blink a couple of times and tilt the photo toward the light. The woman is beautiful, and her smile is amazing. She's a blonde version of Bristol and Darling.

MaryLeigh Treyhune.

Court's haunting.

Even though I'm looking at this picture in shadowed light, I can't miss the fact that her face is surrounded by a mass of blonde hair. Full, thick hair like Bristol and Darling have.

They are their mother's daughters.

"That's MaryLeigh. I met her when I was twenty. We were married in less than two months. Love at first sight, everyone said. She died two years ago."

Okay, so my story seems childish and immature compared to his. Getting dumped for an heiress gal doesn't rate anywhere near death on the scope of losing love.

What do I say to this man? This handsome shell of a man who was once full of life, love and who knows what kind of dreams. Does he now simply exist day to day, minute to minute, with no faith that his life can be full again?

Because Court is clearly just existing.

How do I know?

Because I've been just existing for the past week.

I had no idea it could last so long.

MY FEET POUND THE pavement as sweat runs down my face. Six o'clock in the morning usually doesn't feel like this in Atlanta. Maybe I'll try for five tomorrow morning.

Everything feels so weird. I'm not used to running alone. Dale and I always ran together. We even had our numbers for the Peachtree Road Race this year. I wonder if he's still going to run it.

Tears mingle with the sweat, but I don't care. I wonder how long it will be before everything doesn't remind me of Dale and the life we shared.

I thought this run would clear my head, not fuel the memories.

Through tear-blurred vision I see I'm almost to the cul-de-sac. As I veer to the right of the gazebo that sits in the grassy area in the middle of the street, I spot a guy running down the driveway of the house next door.

He looks up and nods, heading in the opposite direction. I start up Court's driveway, slowing as I approach the house. I can't wait to take a nice, cool shower.

Wiping the sweat-tear mixture off my face, I push my visor and it falls to the ground. As I bend down to pick it up, I turn and see the guy from next door has stopped and is staring at me.

He waves, then starts his run.

I half-wave back, not that keen on showing a friendly gesture to someone I don't even know. But if he lives in one of these million-dollar mansions, I guess he's okay.

I walk into the house, the cold air causing chill bumps the second I step through the door. Walking down the hall to the kitchen, I'm still breathing hard and know I need to cool down.

"That doesn't look like fun at all."

Court's voice makes me jump. He's standing in the kitchen, a cup in his hand. My shirt sticks to my body, I know my face is flushed, and my eyes are probably puffy from crying.

Good thing Barb isn't matchmaking.

"Coffee?" he asks, raising his cup in the air.

"Ooh, no. I'm going to shower."

He finishes his coffee and sets his cup in the sink. "I didn't know you were a runner. I was about to leave. That wouldn't have been good. Mrs. Stratton doesn't arrive until seven."

I glance at my watch again. Six forty-five. "Do you always leave this early?"

"I do. Actually I'm late. I usually leave at six-thirty. I try to beat my assistant, Susan, in. But if you want to run, I can adjust."

It's a good thing I'm used to long hours. Sounds like his assistant works long hours as well. "It's really muggy out there. I'm going to try for five tomorrow."

"All right. I'll make sure you're back before I leave."

I want to look away from him. I really do. Everything about him reminds me of the life I left behind. His light-blue button-up shirt tucked into gray slacks make me long for the office environment. I keep my eyes open, trying to imprint Court's image in my brain in an attempt to erase Dale's.

As I fail at that, I remember the neighbor. "I saw your neighbor this morning. He waved at me. He's a runner, too, I guess."

"I don't know my neighbors."

That statement is curt and abrupt. "Oh. He waved, so I just thought…"

"They always wave when we see them."

"They?"

"The guy next door. He's always with a blonde gal. Not sure if they're married or what. I gotta run. See you tonight."

He blows past me, his clean scent mixing it up with my sweaty scent. I hear the rumblings of the garage door opening, then moments later it shuts. Mrs. Stratton won't be here for fifteen minutes.

I wonder what time the girls wake up.

Because that's how long I have until this place becomes a madhouse.

MIRRORS

"WHAT DO THE girls normally do during the day?"

Clean and now in need of a cup of that coffee Court had offered earlier, I sip the coffee as Mrs. Stratton prepares breakfast. Court had given me the keys to his second car to use while I am Nannying. Maybe the girls would like to go to the beach.

Cracking an egg on the edge of a bowl using only one hand, Mrs. Stratton doesn't look up. "I try and stay out of their way as much as possible."

I set my cup on the counter top and sit on a bar stool in front of my laptop. "Do you know if they are on any type of schedule?"

She chuckles. "From what I can gather, schedule is a forbidden word in this house. The deceased Mrs. Treyhune, God rest her soul, was against schedules. It's my understanding that even when she homeschooled them, they weren't on a schedule."

Homeschooling? That would be a project.

My inexperience with children is not helping at this point. I'm out of my comfort zone in a mighty way. "Maybe I can begin as if I were tackling a new project. That I have experience with."

"Uh huh." Mrs. Stratton whisks the eggs in the bowl.

"Hey. It could work. Define the goal then lay out the steps to achieve said goal."

"You do that."

Her tone and lack of facial communication clearly state her position. She thinks I'm crazy.

She may not be far off in her thinking, but that only increases my desire to prove her wrong.

I will admit that this whole scenario has the potential to take my mind off Dale and my broken heart. I haven't thought of him in at least fifteen minutes.

"She's still here."

The twins walk into the kitchen. Glancing down at their wrists I see that it is Bristol who makes that comment.

"I'm glad she's here. I like her." Darling smiles my way, and my heart warms a little.

"Pull up a stool girls. Your breakfast is almost ready." Mrs. Stratton's focus stays on her task at hand as the girls shimmy their way onto the bar stools. Neither one of them sits directly next to me.

No, they sit where they can stare at me. Which is what they are doing, their brown eyes wide and questioning.

Their hair is still a mess.

Mrs. Stratton places two glasses of orange juice on the counter. They drink it quickly. She slides a plate in front of each of them before refilling their juice.

Mrs. Stratton then places a plate next to my computer. "Would you like some juice, too?"

"The coffee's good. Thank you."

"Are you going to play on your computer all day?" Bristol's tone is challenging.

"I'm not playing. I'm working."

"Your work is being a babysitter for us. You don't do that on a computer."

It's obvious Bristol starts her day in challenge mode. It's a good thing I'm always up for a good challenge. "There are things relating to the nanny position I can do on the computer."

She frowns. "It's just a reason not to pay attention to us."

"Yeah." Darling's chiming in leads me to believe Bristol is in charge of these two.

"Wrong. Working on the computer is actually going to allow me to spend more time with you."

I take a bite of my yummy eggs. One thing is for sure. I'm going to eat well here.

The silence of us all eating is broken by the sound of the garage door opening. Now Mrs. Stratton turns to me with a puzzled expression.

Listening carefully, I don't hear the door go back down, but I do hear footsteps as they come down the hall. They're strong, and they're moving at a fast pace.

Court walks into the kitchen.

"Daddy!" Both girls scream his name and practically fall off their stools trying to reach him. They embrace him, hugging him tight.

Mrs. Stratton steps closer to me, like we are united or something. I have no idea what is going on, but it's obvious Daddy being here during the day isn't a normal occurrence.

While his arms wrap around his girls, I see concern on his face. Something is wrong.

"Daddy, Daddy." The girls are jumping, clapping their hands. "Are you going to stay home with us today?"

"Girls. I'm excited to see you too. But I need to talk to Mrs. Stratton and Shelby, okay? Can you get dressed? Also, pull out those suitcases Grandma and Grandpa gave you for Christmas."

"Are we going on a trip?" Team Twin's eyes are hopeful as Bristol speaks.

"It's a surprise. Now go."

The girls squeal as they run down the hall.

I can't believe the ping of disappointment I'm feeling. Not on this crazy job twelve hours and Court is taking the kids on a trip?

Leaving me with nothing to do? I wonder how long they'll be gone and if I'm going to get paid.

Court watches the girls flee the kitchen. Only then does he turn toward Mrs. Stratton and me. As he runs his hand through his thick, black hair, I see the distraught expression on his face.

"My father had a heart attack."

As he speaks the words about his father, images of my father come into my mind. I can't imagine how my father is taking this news. He's been a fan of Cal Treyhune before I was even thought of.

"Is he…" Mrs. Stratton asks the question I don't want to ask.

"He's alive." Court's voice is soft. "I don't want to tell the girls right now. But we need to go to North Carolina. Storm's sending the plane. We're scheduled to leave at one."

"I can help the girls pack." I slide off the stool, grabbing my coffee.

"You need to pack for yourself too."

I set my coffee back on the counter. "What?"

"I need you to come with us. I'm going to have to focus on my father."

My business brain starts working. Logically. Rationally. "Why don't I stay here with the girls? Then you can truly focus on your father."

"My mom specifically asked for the twins to come. She said she knows Dad will want to see them when he, when he…"

He doesn't finish his sentence, but stalks out of the room.

Looks like I'm going to North Carolina.

"GIRLS, GIRLS, SETTLE down. It's just a car."

But it's really not just a car. It's a limo. A luxurious limo, one I would have given anything to ride in when I was their age.

I secure Darling's seat belt, before clicking my own into place. Team Twin act like they've never been on a trip before.

Maybe they haven't. I have no idea. But my guess is they're not strangers to traveling.

Even though Court is in the limo, he's miles away. The girls are too young to discern the pain on his face, but I can see it.

It mirrors my heart.

When he's not staring out of the window, he's texting or talking on his phone. Talking in hushed tones so the girls don't hear.

But I do.

I learn Storm is Cal's right-hand man. Used to be his crew chief back in the glory days. It seems Storm and Cal Treyhune were bass fishing when Cal had his heart attack. He's in a regional hospital in the northern part of North Carolina.

The drive to the airport doesn't take long. The driver opens the door and Court motions for me to go first as he helps the girls unbuckle their seatbelts.

I step out of the limo to flashes and questions. "How's Cal? Have you talked to him?"

The questions and flashes stop as murmurs of "who's that?" mumble through the throng of paparazzi that would surround the car if the metal barricades hadn't been set up.

Bristol exits the car, Darling right behind her. Flashes start going off and increase if possible as Court steps out of the car. He doesn't say anything as he scoops all three of us in front of him. "Just walk and don't say anything," he says.

We make it into the small airport. Within minutes we are on the plane. Having never been in a private plane before, I would, under normal circumstances, be enamored by all the luxury surrounding me. I've dreamed of being in the midst of such grandness. But I want the grandness to belong to me. I don't want to be employed by the grandness.

At least I can set a standard now of what I would need in a private plane were I to ever own one.

The girls are settling into their seats, excited to be on the plane. They each want their own seat, so Court and I take the bench seat.

"Any more news?" I whisper so the girls don't hear. Although, in my opinion, if a similar group of paparazzi are going to descend on us at the North Carolina airport, he needs to say something to them.

"No. Still the same."

"When are you going to tell the girls?"

He shuts his phone off. When he looks at me, I ache with the pain I see in his eyes.

"Before we land."

"Daddy, why aren't you flying the plane?" Bristol asks.

Court snaps his seat belt. "Because Mr. Murdock is the pilot today."

"I like it when you fly, Daddy." Darling shrugs her shoulders as she smiles.

So yes, they've been on trips.

As soon as we are in the air, the girls occupy themselves with their electronic devices.

Court settles in the seat, his head resting against the back of the soft, tan leather. His eyes close, showcasing his long dark lashes. I take this opportunity, while no one is paying me any attention, to study this man.

His hair is black, clipped short in the back. Professional looking, while his lips look soft, reminding me of a petal on one of Mama's roses. His closely shaven face isn't very tan, an indication he spends a lot of time indoors.

While his outward appearance says peace, I sense the inner turmoil coursing through him.

I know I would feel the same way if I received a call telling me my father had a heart attack.

"Are you done looking at me?"

I jump as he turns toward me. My face heats. Caught perusing the features of the handsome Court Treyhune.

In detail no less.

"I wish I could tell you everything is going to be all right." As I try to change the subject by shifting the focus to his internal struggles, I scoot to my left after speaking, trying to put as much distance between us as I can. Wearing these seatbelts doesn't help.

He focuses his gaze on me, his eyes revealing nothing about his soul. His dark pools remind me of a wall, one that took years to build.

"That's a first."

"A first?" I ask, surprised by the softness of his tone, after the coldness in his eyes.

He shakes his head slightly, his lips tampering a smirk. "Most people speak empty promises."

The distance between us seems to have shrunk instead of widen. Unless I adjust my seatbelt, I can't move farther away. Somehow, I don't think that it would matter. "Maybe I'm not most people."

"Maybe. We'll see, won't we?"

THE REST OF THE flight is uneventful. On the surface, that is. I have many questions warring within me. Court has taken this time to shut his eyes and apparently relax a little. The girls have been watching a movie.

Which left me time to think about the crazy that has happened in the last twenty-four hours.

While I've always wanted luxuries like flying on a private plane, I've never envisioned riding on one with one of racing's greatest. Or rather the son of one of racing's greatest.

And now, racing's greatest is in a hospital in the northern parts of North Carolina fighting for his life.

Court straightens and stretches. My eyes widen and gawk. I'll admit he's eye candy at its finest. Extra sweet. But oh, the issues.

And the heartbreak.

And the twins.

They have been good on this flight. I wonder if somehow they sense their father's sadness.

Court unfastens his seatbelt and breaches the short space between us and the girls. He taps Bristol and motions for them to take their headphones off.

After a bit of whining about how the movie is almost over, they do as he says.

As we start our descent, Court starts his explanation about Cal's, Grandpa Cal's, heart attack.

"Is Grandpa going to be all right?" Bristol asks.

Court's struggle to answer is obvious. I remember his words about empty promises.

What kind of promise, if any, is he going to make to his daughters?

MERCY

"HE IS GOING TO be all right, isn't he, Daddy? He's not going to die like Mommy, is he?" Darling's plea tugs at my heart, and I've just met this child. I can't imagine what is going through Court's heart.

Court starts to speak, then stops, his struggle evident.

"I bet your Grandpa can't wait to see you," I offer, attempting to give Court some time.

The girls smile. I should have used this down time on the plane to brush and untangle their hair instead of Court-gazing. I possess mad skills in French braiding and creating cute buns that my hairdresser friend, Lana, taught me.

The hair will have to wait.

I'm not sure if Court is going to say more, but the wheels of the plane hit the runway, taking the focus off the conversation and putting it on the next leg of the journey.

As we exit the plane, I quickly discern the difference between being somebody important and somebody unimportant.

The details.

We don't have to worry about retrieving our luggage, or renting a car. We simply walk off of the plane to a waiting SUV, the luggage already loaded into the back.

We are each given a bottle of chilled water as well.

I must admit it's nice traveling with the important.

The girls fall asleep in the car as we drive. We turn off the main road, and traverse some winding, often one-lane, back roads. The trees are thick, the signs of human life scattered sparsely throughout.

A small sign welcomes us to Bear's Cave, North Carolina.

"Bear's Cave?" I realize I speak my question out loud.

"Yeah. Dad's had a place here for a long time. Quiet, secluded. Good fishing."

"And bears?"

Court keeps his eyes on the road. "I've never seen any."

That answer doesn't totally comfort me. "It must be called Bear's Cave for a reason."

"Maybe because it's surrounded by the dark forest. Cave-like."

I like how he takes the focus off the bear aspect. "You've obviously been here before."

He continues to keep his gaze on the road, but the blinking of his long, dark lashes doesn't escape my notice.

"Many times. It's Dad's home away from home. He and Storm come here a lot."

"So, it's more like a man cave than a bear cave."

The corner of his mouth turns up, but refuses to go full smile. "Guess so."

Court turns into a driveway and we travel up a slight incline, the gravelly dirt crunching under the tires.

"We're here." The sound of Team Twin's voices brings an air of exuberance to the otherwise somber atmosphere.

The click of seatbelts unfastening is followed by the girls singing, "We're gonna see Grandpa Cal. We're gonna see Grandpa Cal."

Court turns off the SUV and twists his body as best he can in the car to face Bristol and Darling in the back seat. "Girls. Grandpa Cal isn't here. Remember, he's in the hospital."

"Oh, yeah." Their tone, now dejected, raises up the somber atmosphere once again.

"As soon as he's well enough, you can go and visit. Until then, we're hanging out here. Grandma Vera will be here later."

I'm thinking thoughts like this. If Grandma Vera meets me, the new nanny, and sees these girls with their hair in such a mess, she's not going to think me too much of a nanny. Which I'm not, but does it have to be broadcasted?

Then I remember that her husband has had a heart attack, and lucky me, she probably won't even notice their hair.

We all climb out of the car, the fact that we're not in Florida evident by the lack of thick in the air. Sunlight filters through the boughs dense with leaves that grace the still trees. Walking on pine straw and leaves, we make our way to the front door.

The stillness surrounding us amplifies as Court unlocks the door, its low creak as he opens it slicing through the air like a scream in the night.

Slants of sunlight filtering through the windows dot the otherwise dark home.

"It's small," Court says, "but it's home for the next few days."

He starts flipping on lights and the girls run out of the French doors at the back of the living room. I watch as they plop themselves onto the bench swing that hangs from the roof overhanging the deck.

"If you don't mind sharing a room with the twins, there's a pull out couch in there. I'll let Mom have Dad's room and I'll sleep on the one of the couches in the living room."

"That sounds okay." My back aches at the thought of sleeping on the pull-out, but I don't have a choice. This is being a nanny in true form, but somehow I don't feel like more of a nanny.

"I'll grab the luggage. You can stay here with Bristol and Darling, I'll go see Dad."

"No problem. It's what I'm paid to do, right?"

His journey to the front door stops, he turns to look at me. "Absolutely."

The door creaks again when he opens it. No one's entering or exiting this place without an audience. Moments later, he brings in our luggage, depositing mine and the girls' into one of the bedrooms.

"What about food?" I ask as he enters the living area. "The girls are bound to be hungry. It's almost dinnertime."

"These cupboards stay stocked. I'm sure there's something in there for them to eat. Take an inventory. Text me with a list of things you think we need."

I make sure I have his cell number stored.

He walks out to the deck and gives the girls kisses before he leaves. I watch as they smile and light up around Court. Bristol wraps her arms around his neck and doesn't let go. Their playfulness is endearing, and I wonder if what I witnessed yesterday, the tearing through the house screaming, isn't their normal behavior.

Although the nanny, Tracy, did quit.

Said she was done.

Maybe she wasn't a good nanny.

Maybe they see that I mean business and won't put up with their tantrums.

Yeah. That's it. If you lay down the law early enough, they understand who's the boss.

Tracy probably didn't have that insight. Well, she was young. I'm glad I'm older and have some skill sets. It's obviously a plus in this job.

"IF YOU TWO DON'T stop fighting, I'm going to put you in time out."

Court is probably not off this mountain yet and these girls are warring. Bristol accused Darling of swinging the swing too fast. Moments later the complaint was Darling had slowed down too much.

Then war broke out.

After a failed attempt at separating the two, I finally settle them on the couch, at opposite ends. But within moments they are glued to each other in the middle, arms crossed, faces tear-streaked, that hair still a tangled mess around their faces.

Nanny 101 where are you?

"Are you hungry?" Maybe food will take their minds off screaming and fighting.

"No."

"Yes."

Since the wrists with the bands are buried in their armpits I can't tell which one is hungry and which one isn't, but it doesn't matter. They both need to eat.

"Stay here. I'll fix something."

I wander to the kitchen, opening the first door that I'm guessing would be the pantry. My guess is right. There are plenty of canned goods. I slide my gaze past canned sardines, Vienna sausages, and potted meat. If I won't eat it, I'm not giving it to the girls.

I spy some tuna and grab a can.

Opening the refrigerator I see eggs and mayonnaise among other items of food. As I boil the eggs, I find a loaf of bread and couple bags of chips.

This will work.

Encouraged by the silence of the girls, I mix all the fixings together to make tuna salad. I spread the mixture on the bread, and after securing two plates I place some chips on each plate between the sandwich that I had cut in half, at an angle even.

The presentation is nice.

I set the plates on the table and walk to the couch.

My breath hitches at the sight of Bristol and Darling asleep in each other's arms.

"They look like angels when they're sleeping, don't they?"

I jump at the feminine voice. A very nicely attired older woman has just walked in the front door.

The door I didn't hear creak.

This must be Court's mother.

Her grayish blonde hair is styled in a cute, short style. Her clothes look expensive and probably are.

Her face? Worry is etched across an aging, yet beautiful face. With all their money you know she could have work done, but it doesn't look like she has.

Her angels-sleeping comment flutters through my brain. "Yes, they do."

"Then the horns come out when they're awake. Mercy." She pushes the door behind her, then sets her Coach purse on one of the bar stools.

Heading into the kitchen, she stops at the table and points to one of the plates. "Do you mind?"

"No. Not at all."

She slides into the chair and bows her head momentarily. Placing the napkin I had set on the table into her lap, she picks up a chip. Tears glisten in her eyes.

I feel awkward with a capital A.

"Please sit. It's good to have another female to talk to." She motions toward the direction of the other plate.

Heading toward the awkward with a capital A, I slip into the chair.

"I'm Vera Treyhune. And I'm assuming you're the new nanny."

"I am. Shelby Madison. It's nice to meet you."

"You sure are a pretty thing. Court loves beauty. It's interesting

33

though. You're the exact opposite of MaryLeigh with your dark hair, brown eyes and fair skin. Her hair was blonder than blonde, her eyes bluer than blue and her skin tanner than tan. All of which were accentuated by hair coloring, blue contacts and tanning beds."

Her tone doesn't give away her feelings for Court's deceased wife. Vera speaks like she's spouting off a list. "My friend recommended me for the job. I actually thought it was a housekeeping job. I really—" I stop short of telling her I have no experience with children.

Vera Treyhune already has too many things to worry about.

"The girls hate tuna." She places a small bite of the sandwich in her mouth.

Very dainty. I notice her fingernails are polished to perfection. Everything about her looks expensive, feminine, and well put together. "That's good to know."

"I guess you don't usually do the cooking. That would be Mrs. Stratton's job. And you are new."

Again, there is nothing judgmental about her tone. Simply factual. I take a bite of my sandwich, squelching comments regarding how out of my comfort zone I am. I took the job; I need to act like I know what I'm doing.

Do I ask this woman, whom I've just met, how her husband, whom I never met, is doing? Is that proper?

"Cal loves tuna." She breaks her chip in two now. "He likes a little onion and a lot of relish in it."

I take a bite thinking how he wouldn't be liking my tuna too much. I'm also thinking this is a good segue into finding out Cal's condition. "Has anything changed? With Cal?"

With Cal. Like I know Cal. Like he's my friend. Like my father wouldn't give his left lung to be able to ask that question to the Queen of NASCAR, Vera Treyhune.

"No. Still the same. But I have faith. It's the only thing that is keeping me going right now."

I don't have a response for her.

She's my Jesusy mom and NASCAR dad all rolled into one.

Can life become any more ironic?

MOONLIGHT

"THAT WAS A nightmare," Court says, walking in the door.

"Daddy!"

The girls run to him, well energized after the spaghetti dinner that Vera made them before she left to go back to the hospital.

"What was a nightmare?" I hope Cal didn't take a bad turn.

Court hugs Bristol and Darling but looks at me. "The hospital. It's crawling with reporters, cameramen. I knew it would be, but until this morning I had forgotten what it feels like to have a microphone shoved in your face every time you walk out of the door."

"You need to get used to it, my friend. It's where you belong."

I look toward the door. The doorframe is swallowed by a man. And not just any man.

This guy is handsome.

He's magazine-cover handsome.

And apparently he's a friend of Court's.

"Uncle Jared!"

The girls race over to Jared who scoops them up in his arms and spins a couple of circles.

I become dizzy watching, grabbing onto the back of the couch. I also snag a whiff of his cologne.

More than a whiff, actually.

The overpowering scent has me feeling the beginning of a headache. A man wearing too much cologne has always made me wary. Like he's trying to cover up something else.

Or he's prone to excess.

Which one is Jared?

Jared places a kiss on each of their foreheads before setting them down.

What moments ago I envisioned as the time for the girls to settle down before going to bed has just been uprooted and turned upside down.

As much of an uproar Jared creates with his bold appearance and wild actions, Court creates the same level of disruption, only in a much quieter way.

Everything about Court is distinct and deliberate.

And there's an air of mystery about him that sets him apart from other guys.

Guys.

It now comes to my attention that I haven't thought of Dale in quite a while. Ever since Vera arrived. Between visiting with her and helping with the girls' dinner, I haven't had a free moment to dwell on my lost love.

Either Dale's image is fading in my mind, or it's paling in comparison to the two men in this room.

A part of me still aches at the loss I feel at not having Dale in my life. When you've shared everything with one person for a long time, it's hard having no one to automatically turn to.

Of course Dale wouldn't understand any of this. Not being able to tell two ten-year-old girls apart. Not knowing what to say to a man whose father is in ICU and to see him he has to contend with reporters and cameramen. All whose agenda is waiting to capture a tortured expression on Court's face, or report the lack of one if it isn't there.

Jared looks at me. "I'm Jared James."

"Shelby Madison."

"Court. Holding out on me, are you?" Jared's grin is mischievous, reminding me of Bristol and Darling.

"Jared, Shelby is the new nanny. Remember I told you about her when you arrived at the hospital." Court turns to me. "Shelby, Jared is a long-time friend and CFO of TAG."

"Tag?" I ask.

"Treyhune Automotive Group." Court looks at the girls. "What's for dinner?"

"Spaghetti. But we ate it all." Bristol crosses her arms.

"Ate it all?" Court walks to the kitchen. "What's a poor dad to eat, then?"

"Yeah, and poor Uncle Jared." Jared walks into the kitchen area with

Court. The girls are right behind them, but I stay put on the living room side of the bar, still able to see what's happening in the kitchen but a safe distance away from all that testosterone.

And all that CFO-ness. Disappointment at the loss of the livelihood I had such a passion for creeps in.

"I appreciate you coming, Jared." Court rummages through the pantry.

"No problem. Cal's like my dad, too."

"I know." Court sets a box of crackers and a jar of peanut butter on the counter.

Jared grabs two knives from a drawer, making it obvious he's spent some time here at the man cave, and hands one to Court.

"Is that what you guys call dinner?" I ask.

Court smiles. "Not necessarily, but it sums up the extent of my cooking skills."

"Ditto." Jared shoves a cracker topped with peanut butter into his mouth.

The willingness of these guys to settle for this makeshift dinner warms my heart. Without thinking too much about it, because I know I will talk myself out of it, I walk to the freezer. Spying a cut up chicken, I put it into the microwave, set the defrost setting, and push start.

Shooing the guys and the girls out of the kitchen, I plop a bag of flour, salt and a can of pepper onto the counter.

Searching the pantry once again, I set out two cans of corn, then grab two cans of potatoes. "Canned potatoes aren't the best but they'll have to do."

Looking deep into the refrigerator, I spy a roll of biscuits in the back, close to expiring, but they'll work.

Saying goodbye to Shelby R. Madison, CFO, I reach back into time and pull out everything Shelby Ray Madison knows about southern cooking.

I push up my shirt sleeves, wash my hands, and dive into the past I've tried so hard to lose.

UNABLE TO SLEEP, I slip out of the room I'm sharing with the girls, hoping I don't wake Court or Jared who are bunked out in the living room.

I slowly open the back door to the deck, making no sound as I exit. Even in June, the night is cool. I rub my arms wishing I had worn pajamas with long sleeves.

Settling on the swing, I keep it steady as to not make any noise. The full moon slices a pale light through the thick forest of trees. The sounds of the night that surround the cabin make me happy the deck is high off the ground. I feel safer.

Not that I'm worried about bears or anything.

Hearing the door open, I hold my breath, wondering who will walk outside. Surely I didn't wake anyone.

Court's lean, yet strong-looking frame steps onto the porch, his gaze turning immediately toward me. "I thought you came out here."

His voice is soft, the very opposite of his appearance.

My bare feet push against the wooden deck, holding the swing steady. "I didn't mean to wake you."

He walks to the railing, leaning on it with both hands and staring into the night. Into the darkness. "You didn't. I couldn't sleep. I had just decided to come out here when I saw you walk by. I hope you don't mind."

"No. Sometimes I have a hard time adjusting to new places." Especially after showing my country-roots upbringing in that fried chicken, mashed potatoes, biscuits and gravy dinner I prepared.

What was I thinking? I hadn't cooked like that in years. Dale didn't even know I could cook like that. But he was always taking me out or catering in. Besides, with working late every night I had no time to cook.

"I have a hard time adjusting to the fact that my father had a heart attack."

I know he didn't intentionally make my problem seem lame, but he made my problem seem lame. "I give. Your adjustment is harder."

He turns and looks my way. "I didn't mean that the way it sounded. I'm sorry. I'm not thinking clearly right now."

"It's okay." And really it is.

As he walks toward me, I want to reiterate that it is indeed okay. He doesn't need to be close to make amends.

"Mind if I join you?" He nods toward the swing.

Would it matter if I did, I wonder? "No."

The swing creaks with his weight, the space between us almost nonexistent. The air has somehow warmed, and I'm betting I couldn't conjure up an image of Dale if I tried.

Court's presence swallows anything that isn't who he is.

"My mom likes you."

I'm unprepared for his statement. "I like her, too."

"She's strong. She'll pull my dad through this."

I thought about the faith Vera said she had. And the statement Court made about not having faith in anything.

Yet they both are hoping for the same result.

"How long have they been married?"

"Thirty-five years. I'm the honeymoon baby."

I laugh. "We have something in common. I'm the honeymoon baby, too."

"Brothers or sisters?" He starts the swing moving slowly.

"No. You?"

"No. I'm the proverbial spoiled only child."

I shake my head. "Only child, yes. Spoiled. No." I think back to my childhood. Court and I would have never hung in the same circles.

Ever.

Visions of my homemade clothes, thrift-store shoes and used toys always had me wanting the finer things in life. I finally acquired the finer things.

And my life is at its lowest point.

How did this happen?

I have two-plus months to regroup.

"Did you grow up in Atlanta?" he asks.

To him his question is simple. To me it's the beginning of a barrage of questions that I don't want to answer. "A little north of the city. And you?"

Even though I know he grew up in North Carolina, I want to switch the focus off my upbringing.

"North Carolina. I bought the house in Florida about three years ago. I miss it here. Do you miss Atlanta?"

Not wanting to answer, but not wanting to be rude either, I open my mouth to speak but am saved by the sound of the door opening.

"Whoa." Jared's voice breaks through the night. "I'm not interrupting anything, am I?"

He points his index finger at Court, then me, then back at Court.

I want to jump up and hug him for interrupting. "No."

"So, you two…just friends? Not sure I'm buying it."

"Buy it." Court's tone has a clipped sound to it now.

"Don't have to tell me twice." Jared grabs a chair and pulls it up close to the swing. "Why don't you trade places with me? You may not be in the market for a pretty lady, but I am. And a cozy deck under the moonlight is a

great place to start."

MADNESS

MY SLOWLY-LOSING-sight-of-my-ex-fiancé-Dale mind is flattered at the CFO's attention. Flattered and uncomfortable. I barely know Court, am in charge of his children and am being hit on by his friend and business associate.

And his cologne.

Last week at this time I was crying in my drink at the bar with Barb. Now look at me. Moonlight madness in North Carolina.

With two very attractive men.

But again, awkward position. "Actually, I was on my way in. See you guys in the morning."

I walk past scents of men, cologne, and the pine in the air. I am not at all tired but want out of this situation.

I'm still much too brokenhearted to even think about another man in a romantic way.

Aren't I?

WEDNESDAY MORNING came early with Bristol and Darling waking me up with the sound of them fighting.

"Break it up you two." My still sleepy voice holds no authority whatsoever.

And they know this.

We all tumble out of bed, taking turns in the bathroom. It's hopeless for me to think the household will not be woken by our rumblings. Bristol and Darling don't know the meaning of the word quiet.

Unless they are asleep.

I scoot out to the kitchen scrambling to brew some coffee. Both couches are empty, and I wonder where Court and Jared are. I glance out on the deck to find it empty.

Finding everything I need, I start a pot of coffee and look for some cereal for the girls.

I come up with nothing.

The front door bursts open and Court and Jared come in, laughing.

Jared points at me. "Awake. I win."

Court rolls his eyes and shakes his head. "You got lucky." He turns his attention to me. "We brought donuts."

He sets a white box on the counter. Through a clear window I see all different kinds of fun toppings.

"Okay, great." I shake my head. No wonder the girls are always on the run. They live on sugar.

"Oh, here." Jared hands Court some cash. "Before I forget. I went to the ATM while you were buying the donuts. I have no idea why my card wouldn't work to book my flight yesterday."

Court pockets the money. "Thanks. Maybe a glitch or something with the online process. That's happened to me before."

"Maybe." Jared doesn't look so sure.

Court taps the donut box. "I brought donuts because we are celebrating."

"Celebrating?" I ask.

"Yes. In a big way. Mom called about an hour ago. Dad's awake and the doctors say everything looks like it's going to be okay. She's on her way here, and then Jared and I are going to head over. I think it's still too soon to take the girls."

Ah. Donuts and lighter mood explained. "Probably," I agree. "They'll be happy to know they can see their grandpa soon, though."

Jared grabs one of the donuts. "Court. The more I think about it, why don't you go on? We kid about me being family, but I think it'd be too much for both of us to go at once. I'll take the car and see Cal later tonight."

I wonder if Jared notices the strange look that passes across Court's eyes. If he does, he doesn't say anything.

"Whatever. I know Dad would love to see you."

Jared slides onto a bar stool. "You tell him I'll be there tonight."

Bristol and Darling run into the kitchen. They are beyond thrilled at the sight of the donuts. Court, the girls and I sit at the breakfast table in the kitchen, while Jared stays perched on the bar stool, like he's our overlord or something.

I can't help but be taken in by Jared's good looks. His personality seems fun and exciting, and life is probably a constant party when he's around. But there's a look in his eyes that I can't figure out. There's hesitancy at times that I'm not sure if I'm imagining or not.

Court washes his hands. "Mom should be here any minute. I'll go ahead and leave. When I return, we'll make a game plan regarding the rest of the week and the weekend. If he's doing okay, we'll probably head out of here in a couple of days."

The girls groan but don't protest too much.

Court isn't gone fifteen minutes when Vera comes in the door. She's not alone this time. An older man is with her. He literally looks like he could sleep while he stands.

"Jared," Vera says, hugging Court's friend. "I'm so glad you're here. Court really needs you right now."

"You know I wouldn't be anywhere else." Jared's tone is compassionate.

"Storm, man, you're looking rough." Jared breaks his hug with Vera to shake the man's hand.

"You would be too if it was Court in that hospital bed." The man Jared called Storm looks my way, a puzzled expression on his face.

"Hi. I'm Shelby, Bristol and Darling's nanny. It's nice to meet you."

"Shelby. Nice name. Brings back some fond memories, but lucky for you I'm too tired to recall any of them. I'm gonna pull up a couch and sleep for a spell. 'Night, y'all."

After procuring a blanket and a pillow for Storm, Vera announces that she is going to sleep as well and heads back to Cal's room.

Bristol, Darling and their pent up energy aren't a good combination for two sleeping adults. "Do you know if there is a park nearby? It would do these girls good if we could go outside for a while."

Jared winks at me. Like we have some secret. Again, the flattery-awkward feeling returns. I decide I'm not over Dale enough to be flirting with anyone. That's where the strange sensation originates.

I wonder how long that will last.

"I don't know about a park, but there are walking trails. They could run off some energy by doing some hiking."

"Are the trails well marked? I'm not sure about venturing too far off."

"They are, but we'll all go. Come on." He opens the door and waves his hand for me and the girls to go outside. "Let's walk."

Bristol and Darling have to be told three times not to run too far ahead. They finally settle into a rhythm that matches mine and Jared's.

"You know, I can't picture a pretty girl like you wanting to be a nanny. Why do you want to hide away with little kids all day?"

I debate on how much of my story to tell him. Would he be fascinated to know that just a short time ago I myself was a CFO? Of course, Dale's company wasn't nearly as big as Treyhune Automotive, but the responsibilities had to be close to being the same.

I never realized the pressure I was under to make a profit until I was no longer under the pressure. It had become a normal way of life.

"I don't see it as hiding. I'm taking a different direction in life for a little while."

"Shelby! Watch!"

Bristol kicks a pine cone to Darling, and they start playing like it's a soccer ball. Bristol looks over her shoulder, I guess to make sure I'm watching. I wave at her and smile. "I'm glad you're having fun."

"So," Jared continues. "You're a lady of mystery."

I look at him and raise my eyebrows. "Mystery?"

"You're not real forthcoming with information."

His hands are in his pockets, his smile is warm, and his face is beautiful. I wonder why his eyes tell a different story. Maybe they're hanging out with his scent.

I'm not keen on relaying my past to anyone, much less these people I've just met. "There's not much to know. I'm a simple girl."

He laughs. "Nobody who looks like you is simple."

I'm not sure why he's trying to press information from me. Maybe he wants to have a topic of conversation. "How about I *try* my best to keep it simple."

"Now that I can believe. We all would like things to be simple, but somehow they end up being so complicated and out of control that it becomes ridiculous."

His tone takes on a wild edge, and I wonder what is driving his statement.

I try to look at him, but he's intent on staring straight ahead. Bristol and Darling are still kicking that pine cone.

And their hair is still a mess.

Maybe when we get back I can tackle it with a brush.

"I do have a question for you."

He now turns my way, his face calm, his gaze searching. "Yes?"

"Why is this town called Bear's Cave?"

Shrugging his shoulders, he kicks a stick that is apparently in his way. A few strands of pine straw fly along with it. "Not sure. Maybe because there are bears here?"

His answer clearly says he has no clue. "No old town legends or anything, huh?"

"Not that I know of. Now Storm, when he's awake and running on full steam, he might be able to tell you about any legends. Shoot, he is a legend."

Jared's tone is back to normal now. The wildness about him has diminished, leaving me more than curious about him.

But again, my heart can't go where he is.

Not now.

It's a good thing we've got two kids in tow.

WE ARRIVE BACK at the house to full-blown chaos.

Chaos that doesn't seem to be bothering Storm, as he's snoring loudly on the couch.

Vera, who apparently didn't sleep long, is talking to another lady, who appears to be in her forties, maybe. She's very attractive, thin, and stylishly dressed. And there are three children, ranging from what looks to be about ten to fifteen, ransacking the kitchen looking for who knows what.

Vera stands. "There you are. We were beginning to worry about you."

Bristol and Darling spy the other kids and take off screaming into the kitchen. The two girls in the kitchen scream as well, and all the girls start hugging. The boy, who looks to be the oldest, stands off to the side, looking thoroughly annoyed.

He grabs a bag of chips off the counter, shoves his hand into the bag, then fills his mouth with a handful of chips.

"This is my youngest sister, Crystal," Vera says. "Much younger. Almost twenty years between us. Crystal, this is Shelby, Bristol and Darling's new nanny, and you know Jared, of course."

"Good to see you again, Jared. So nice of you to come up here to be with Court. He needs good friends right now. Shelby, it's nice to meet you. How long have you been the girls' nanny?"

The question is getting old. How many nannies do they go through? I'm beginning to wonder at the sanity of taking this job. Does everyone think I'm insane?

"Just started." Goodness. Cooking fried chicken last night and now I'm speaking in incomplete sentences.

"I'm sure you'll do fine." Crystal looks at Vera as she speaks. "Especially if our plan works out."

Plan? Did they make plans for me?

"We'll wait until Court gets back then run everything by him. I'm heading back to the hospital right after he gets here." Vera's tone has hope in it.

As long as Court is around he will make the decisions. I understand that, but if the plans involve me, can't I be a part of making them? This is further proof I have no business being a nanny. I'm used to being the planner, not the plannee.

"These are your children?" I ask Crystal, nodding toward the kitchen.

"Yes. Davey, the only boy and the oldest. The twins, my twins, are Taylor and Saylor. They're the same age as Bristol and Darling."

Did I hear right? Taylor and Saylor?

Oh, and their hair! Taylor and Saylor's hair is pulled back into neat ponytails, curled at the ends. Each has a big white bow covering up any ponytail holders. Standing next to them, my twins' hair looks like rat nests. If only I could get the pony-tail holders off their wrists and into their hair.

"We live about an hour away," Crystal continues. "My husband works at Treyhune Motorsports. He's in Michigan with the team now. We were all supposed to fly out there, because you know Sunday is Father's Day. But the plans have changed."

Father's Day. I forgot. I need to put a card in the mail. I will need to make a phone call. And possibly lie.

The front door creaks open and Court walks in. Squeals from Bristol and Darling are contagious as Taylor and Saylor squeal right along with them, all four rushing Court.

Davey hangs in the kitchen, still shoving chips in his mouth.

Meanwhile, Storm is still snoring away on the couch.

Unbelievable.

This man-cave get-away fishing cabin is in no way equipped to house all these people. Six adults and five kids overwhelm this place.

Crystal grabs the bag of chips from Davey. "Davey, take the girls outside. The adults need to talk. And remember, stay right out front."

Davey, grumbles and has a sour look on his face, but he complies. The girls beat him to the door and giggle their way out.

Court gives an update on his father, and when he reveals that Cal will be home by the weekend, the guys high-five each other while the women shed tears.

"God has certainly answered our prayers." Vera hugs Crystal before hugging Court. "God is faithful, Court. He is. You have to have faith."

I see Court stiffen as his mother speaks. He doesn't reply or answer or in any way acknowledge that she said anything.

Jared's eyes shift between Court and Vera as she speaks, like he's waiting for something to happen. Something unfavorable.

Or maybe the conversation is making him uncomfortable.

Maybe I'm just trying to find reasons not to be attracted to the CFO. I might have a lot in common with him, but my heart doesn't want to go on a romantic journey right now.

Maybe never again.

I think I need to leave Jared and his possible dispositions alone and concentrate on being a nanny.

You know, what I was hired to do.

At Vera's suggestion, we all sit around the table where she and Crystal lay out their plans. Their plans which include Crystal taking Bristol and Darling for the rest of the week.

I want to shout no! Because then what would I, the nanny, do for those few days?

With an eye on Court, I watch as his facial expression doesn't change much. Jared has sequestered himself very close to me, which happens to be the furthest away from the conversation. Truth be told, he's not involved in this anyway.

Maybe I will go with Crystal and all the kids.

That thought scares me.

"Sounds like a good plan." Court taps his fingers on the table as he speaks. "There are some things going on at the dealerships I need to look into. And there is a meeting Friday morning that I need to be in if at all possible."

"So, it's settled, then." Vera smiles. "Crystal will take all the kids to her house, I'll get Cal home and settled in. Court you do what you need to do then meet us at the house on Sunday. We'll have a huge Father's Day celebration."

Court excuses himself to call the guy about getting the plane ready.

I look at Crystal. "I didn't pack very many clothes for the girls."

"That's okay," Crystal replies. "They wear the same size as my girls. There'll be no lack of clothing."

"Great." Do I sound concerned like a nanny should? I'm not sure where I fit into this scenario. There wasn't any mention of me going to Crystal's.

"Gotta love this, don't you." I feel warmth on my shoulder and realize Court is standing behind me, his hand on my shoulder. "Work a couple of days and get a vacation."

I guess that means I'm not going with Crystal, Bristol, Darling and the rest of the crew. "You're the boss."

He squeezes my shoulder and I try to unsqueeze my heart. "We'll be leaving in about an hour, so I guess we need to pack up and get ready to go. You, too slug."

Jared laughs and tips back in his chair. "On it. I'll be ready."

Jared winks at me as Court's hand slips from my shoulder.

As the warmth leaves I realize I like the warmth better than the wink.

MOMENT

TWO HOURS LATER I step back onto Court's plane. He had opted once again not to play pilot, so I settle myself in the same place as I had when we flew up to North Carolina with the girls.

But instead of Court taking the seat next to me, Jared sits down and pats my knee. He seems to have lightened the cologne level today. The distinct scent is still there, just not as strong.

"This is nice." After speaking he takes his hand away from my jean-clad leg before I can protest it being there in the first place.

Before Court can witness his gesture.

I shake my head and turn my gaze away from Jared. Not being able to discern if my reactions are overreactions is driving me crazy. Am I sour to the touch of another man?

I spent many nights in Dale's arms. We shared kisses that I thought were the most passionate ever in the world kisses.

Then I remember Court's touch. The warmth I felt on my shoulder as his hand rested there. I didn't overreact then.

As the plane takes off I redirect my thinking. I have a temporary nanny job in a city far away from my home. At the end of the summer I'll be back in Atlanta, living in my condo. I need to start thinking about securing a real job.

One that will pay my expenses for the lifestyle I was and will continue to be accustomed to.

This little stint with Court and the twins, although unexpected, has only fueled my desire for the nicer things in life. The ability to be on the giving end, not the receiving end.

A life without financial worry is a life of comfort.

Of being accepted.

No aspirations of having my own plane, though. I know where to draw the line in my thinking.

It hasn't escaped my notice that Jared has scooted closer to me. But as nice as he looks and as good as he smells, I find my thoughts, when they aren't on Dale, drifting to Court.

The nice part about Court sitting across from me is that I can look at him. As I do, I catch him looking at me. My gaze quickly shifts away, and I see Jared smiling at me.

I lean my head against the back of the seat and close my eyes. Maybe if I pretend to sleep, Jared will focus his attentions somewhere else. It's not a long flight. Surely I can keep him at bay until we land.

"So," Court says. "I was looking over the financials and a couple of the stores' profits seem to have really dropped over the last couple of months. Nothing stuck out as being wrong, or substantially different. Are you on top of that?"

"Yeah, I am. I've been over at those stores trying to check on the numbers before we run the statements for June. Thought maybe I could stop something from derailing if you know what I mean."

"Do you have your assistant helping? I can't remember her name."

"Janice. Her name is Janice, and uh, she's out on maternity leave, remember?"

Court rubs his forehead. "How could I forget? Susan is swamped. I meant was Janice helping before she left? I think there are some strange things going on."

Court's tone sends shivers up my arms. To rub them would reveal that I'm awake. Whereas I don't think their conversation would be different if they knew I was awake, letting them think I'm taking a nap is okay with me.

"Janice probably doesn't have the skill set needed to help me with this type of issue. Just know I'm keeping an eye on those two stores."

"Okay. Keep me posted on this. It's your job to make sure we're making money. But I do have a question. Why did you hire Janice? It doesn't sound like she can do the job."

"I didn't mean to make it sound like that. She does a great job. But digging into certain accounts and stuff, I just think she wouldn't know what she was looking for. When she comes back from leave, I'll be training her more."

"Okay. If you need Susan's help with that, let me know. Susan is amazing."

I swear I hear Jared sigh. Not loud like Court would know, but a soft one. Kind of like a whew. Like he just passed a test or something.

The rest of the flight passes in silence. All of us taking a break from life right now. Apparently Court has reason to be concerned about his work, this on top of his father's heart attack.

I really have no idea what I'm going to do back at the mansion without Team Twin there. But I guess I'll find out in a couple of hours.

WE ARRIVE AT THE mansion to find Mrs. Stratton already gone since there was no one to cook and clean for. There's a different vibe in the house without Bristol and Darling.

A quiet vibe.

I unpack the few clothes I had taken with me, find the laundry room and start washing clothes. I make my way into the kitchen to look for something to drink. My stomach is rumbling as well, so I scour the refrigerator for dinner ideas.

"I thought we might go out."

The cold air of the refrigerator balances the heat of my face as I realize Court is speaking to me. Why do his words and gazes elicit such a reaction from me?

I straighten and shut the door. "Sure."

I turn around and pretty much bite my lip to keep my mouth from falling open.

This man is gorgeous. There are simply no other words to describe him. Hot is too tame for the likes of Court Treyhune. And yes, just a short time ago, I was engaged. I realize this. But that reality is moving further and further away from my memory.

As is the image of Dale's handsome face.

"I want to discuss something regarding the girls before we go. Do you have time to talk now?"

Other than the load of laundry I've started there isn't too much on my agenda. "Sure." My face almost heats again at the realization that Court probably thinks I have a one-word vocabulary.

"Great. Pull up a bar stool."

Moments later, as we are settled, I do everything in my power to ensure I stay focused on our conversation.

"I want to talk to you about homeschooling the girls."

I straighten and sit back in my chair. "Uh, I have no experience in that area. None." I say this like I have experience in being a nanny.

He shakes his head. "I don't mean you homeschooling them. I would like you to interview people to start homeschooling them when school begins again."

Relief flows through me at his words. "Okay. I'm not sure where to start, but I have the time to figure all that out."

"I have information that MaryLeigh gathered. She never actually homeschooled in Florida. She became too sick too fast. But I'll get it for you tomorrow and you can look through it. It will be a place to start."

"Okay. That would be helpful."

MaryLeigh was insistent that the girls be homeschooled. She did it as long as she could when we lived in North Carolina. I know she's probably aggravated in heaven that I haven't gotten around to handling it yet."

I chuckle. "I don't think aggravation is allowed in heaven."

He does that barely smiling thing again.

Which is a good thing for me. I think Court's full smile is reserved for those he loves, like his mother and his daughters.

"Given MaryLeigh's personality I wouldn't be surprised if she didn't change heaven."

I may not know much about God, but I remember Mama always saying God never changed. He is the same yesterday, today and tomorrow. "Not sure that's possible."

"I'm not talking blasphemy here. I mean she probably turned heaven on its ear. She was anything but docile. Even at the end."

His words aren't an invitation to inquire about MaryLeigh or her death. Which is a relief as I feel at odds discussing anything regarding Court's first wife. His mom's play by play on her looks was weird enough.

And he's vague in his speech. Which is normal. He doesn't know me very well and conversing about his wife, who has passed away, can't be comfortable for him. At least it wouldn't be for me. "Do you have a deadline for this project you've assigned me to?"

"As long as the girls have someone by the time school starts. We can find that date online."

"If they're registered in public school there's probably some paperwork to fill out regarding that."

"Probably. There's so much red tape for everything nowadays."

Before I can respond the doorbell chimes. Court's expression turns puzzled. "Not expecting anybody. I'll be right back."

Moments later I hear voices.

Jared is here.

An expectant, yet troubled sensation races through me.

"Wasn't sure what you had planned for dinner," he says as he walks through the living room into the kitchen. "But I brought a large pizza. Thought we could all dine in together tonight." He slides the box onto the counter.

"All your date prospects busy tonight?" Court asks.

"Funny." Jared opens the refrigerator and holds out a bottle of beer. "Care for one?"

He's looking back and forth between Court and me.

"Okay." Court's response is curt.

"No." I decline this offer to be one of the guys.

"Shelby's a wine kind of girl." Court slides onto the bar stool next to me which leaves Jared no choice but to sit next to Court.

Jared has changed into a dark blue polo shirt that tucks nicely into his jeans. Again, his cologne is overpowering, almost masking the smell of the pizza.

"You've just met and you know what type of girl she is?" Jared's tone is disbelieving.

Neither of us responds. He's obviously familiar with the place as he opens a cabinet and places a plate in front of each of us. He also opens a drawer and grabs some cloth napkins.

He holds the pizza box in front of me, the lid open and inviting.

"The works," he says, nodding at the pizza.

I grab a piece but the cheese is being difficult. As I try to rein it in with my index finger of my other hand, Court has the same idea. Our fingers touch and again that warm feeling comes over me.

"Sorry," we both say at the same time. We also kind of laugh together while Jared stands there with a scowl on his face.

I pull the lone strand of cheese on my pizza while Court grabs a piece from the box.

Jared slides two pieces on his plate before setting the box down and settling himself on the barstool next to Court.

"So, seriously," Court starts. "Who was that brunette you were dating? Are things off with her?"

Jared wipes his mouth with the fancy cloth napkin. "Ansley? I wasn't serious about her. We only went out a couple of times."

"Didn't you take off a Friday a couple of weeks ago to take her to Key West for a long weekend?"

Jared smiles a cocky smile. "Yeah. We had a good time. She's expensive though. A drinker. Seven or eight glasses of wine at ten plus dollars a pop adds up."

Court takes a swig of beer before setting his bottle on the counter. "That's what I pay you the big bucks for, isn't it? To impress the ladies?"

Jared shares a shocked look which we all know is fake. "The salary isn't that big. Besides, if you keep talking like this Shelby will think I'm a player."

"And?" Court shrugs.

"And I'm not. I don't want her getting the wrong idea. She's too pretty to be thinking bad thoughts about me."

I continue eating in silence. It's obvious these guys have a history. One that makes them comfortable bantering back and forth regarding all matters.

I'm not that comfortable yet.

I'm still trying to figure out how to move forward with my life. And at the moment forward looks like having pizza with two handsome men.

This is a good moment.

MEANING

THE NICE MOMENT turns into an awkward evening.

Jared won't leave.

Court has made a couple of comments indicating that he's tired and needs some sleep, but Jared continues to hang out. They talk a lot of racing which at one point I excuse myself from to switch out my laundry.

When I come back the subject has changed to football.

Then it turns to movies, before the subject of concerts came up.

"The Rolling Stones are coming in a couple of weeks," Court says.

"I love the Stones," I add. "I have always wanted to see them."

"Perfect," Jared says. "I have two tickets and need someone to go with me."

"I, uh." I look to Court whose eyes are narrowed and staring at Jared.

"What?" Jared asks me.

"I don't know what I'll be doing. The girls will be back, and I'm not sure of our schedule."

Jared playfully punches Court in the arm. "Come on, buddy. Give your nanny a night off to go and have some fun. And she loves the Stones."

Court takes on an I-don't-care expression and doesn't even look my way. I want to connect with him so I can eye-plead help-me-out-here.

Although, really do I want help? The conversation on the plane keeps replaying in my head, along with Jared's sigh. This might give me a chance to pick Jared's brain about what's going on with the finances at the dealerships. My brain is dying to finagle some numbers.

But it is important for me to make sure Jared doesn't know my background.

Yes, I'm playing sneaky.

It will keep my brain fresh for these three months hanging with the girls.

I catch a quiet, yet soulful gaze from Court. Shaking my head I realize Court is no more soulful over me than I am over him. "Okay. If Court doesn't mind, I'll go."

"Great." Jared stands. "I'd better head home. It's getting late."

I see a relieved expression cross Court's face. Jared, it appears, is immune to people's body language and facial expressions.

"See you later, Jared." Court steps out of the living room toward the front entryway.

"Goodnight," I say, more than ready to call it a night myself and crawl into bed.

"Good night to you, pretty lady." Jared walks over and takes my hand in his. He kisses the back of it gently. I feel my face heat, but not like it does around Court. No, this is from embarrassment. Jared is over the top.

I swear he flicks his tongue on my skin before ending his brushed kiss.

"I can't wait for our date. Ha. I'm a poet." He continues to stare at me as he backs out of the living room.

Way over the top.

And he used the word date. His meaning of going to a concert is different from my meaning of going to a concert.

I thought we were simply going to a concert. So I could pick his brain.

I'm so glad Court is already on his way to the door and doesn't witness the event.

"So, you're here a few days and already dating my best friend, huh?"

Court has good ears. "He called it a date. I didn't."

"Jared always gets the pretty girls."

The only reason Court wouldn't get the pretty girls is if he didn't try. He has everything a woman would want in a man. He's loaded to the brim with all the star qualities in life.

Yet he lives here, still grieving MaryLeigh's death, and works from morning until night.

It's a shame is what it is.

"I'll see you in the morning."

With those words, he walks from the living room to the side of the house where his bedroom and office are.

My heart hitches disappointment that I might have disappointed him by going to the concert with Jared. Certainly he knows I thought it was just a friend thing.

I had no idea Jared would consider it a date.

And I can't tell Court about my mission.

THE FIVE A.M. RUN is a little cooler than the previous run a couple of days ago. I shower and barely finish my first cup of coffee before Court saunters into the kitchen. He pours a cup of coffee for himself then nods to me. "Good morning."

"Good morning."

His hair is still wet from his shower and his soap scent lingers softly in the air, making me think of days spent outdoors, breeze blowing. I love the way he dresses for success in his crisp white shirt, sleeves rolled up, his gray slacks and beautifully classy-looking black shoes.

"Did you run this morning?" he asks, breaking my starefest.

"I did. Still sultry, but slightly cooler."

"Florida's like that. Whenever you're ready, you can come into my office. I have the information about homeschooling."

"I'm ready now." I slide off the bar stool and follow Court.

His office is a manly sort of place with a large fish gracing the top of one of the walls. A big, dark heavy-looking desk and matching office furniture take up a lot of space. There is a small settee with a coffee table in front of it.

"You can sit there if you'd like." He motions toward the settee. There is a box sitting on the coffee table. A box filled with papers.

Court takes a seat in a straight-backed chair in front of his desk. He turns the chair so it faces me. He points to the box. "There are the notes and such."

I widen my eyes and nod toward the box. "In there? All that paper?"

"Yes. I'm not sure how organized it is."

I slide the box to the floor in front of me and fish out the top layers of papers. "I thought all this would be on the computer."

"MaryLeigh wasn't big on computers. She liked tangible stuff. Stuff you could actually hold and touch."

MaryLeigh's tangible stuff preference would make this job harder. "Okay. I'll take this box to the, well, I guess to my room and work on it."

"You can use this space. I'm going to my office. You can use my computer, or your own. Whichever. Also, there's a phone here if you need to make calls." He points to a cordless phone sitting in a charger on his desk.

"Okay. Mrs. Stratton indicated that someone was hired at one point to homeschool the girls. Do you know if that information is in here?"

He shrugs and stands. "Probably. Although they weren't here long." He makes his way behind his desk and leans over for a moment. He looks like he's rifling through a drawer.

After about a minute he holds up file folders. "I knew I had some here. You can use these to organize all the information if you want."

He sets the folders on top of his desk.

I see a printer sitting on a credenza that lines one of the walls. "Is there a scanner on that printer?"

"Yes."

"If I can download the printer drivers to my computer, I'll probably scan the documents straight to my computer if that's okay."

Nodding his head he sips his coffee. "Sure. Whatever works for you. I think the set up disks for the printer are in this credenza somewhere if you don't find what you need online."

"I'll figure it out."

"Okay." As Court comes around his desk he takes another sip of his coffee. Just as he finishes sipping he misjudges his route, and his left leg slams into the desk, spilling the coffee down the front of his white shirt. He leans his body forward, the liquid missing his slacks.

"That's hot." He sets his coffee on his desk and starts unbuttoning his shirt. I don't do anything but stare at his chest as his shirt flies open.

Oh, my.

He untucks it as he walks out of his office, and I am the recipient of six-pack abs.

Talk about face flushing.

I guess this job does have its perks.

THE DAY GOES BY quickly. It takes me quite a while to organize the box of papers, but I do, laying out piles on top of Court's desk. I love how his scent invades this room, and when I move his chair, or fan some papers, I'm reminded of him.

I find more papers of the girls' schoolwork than actual homeschooling information. There are attendance records that don't seem to be filled out correctly, or if they are, the girls didn't get much schooling. There's also a lot of North Carolina information which won't help me at all.

What Florida contact information I find is a couple of years old, but it gives me a place to start. It seems there is a co-op that I can contact and see where to go from there.

Another discovery that I make is that Bristol and Darling have an aptitude for art. Well, I'm assuming it's both of them. There are no names on the artwork, but a lot of the pictures are done twice.

It's interesting, this box. As much as Court's scent invades this room, I catch a fresh, sunny, flowery scent every now and then on the papers.

Vague memories of seeing MaryLeigh with Court on the television when I did have the unfortunate timing of being at home when a race was on, try to make their way into my mind. Visions of blondness and sunglasses are about all I can recall.

Deciding I need to start scanning the documents, I try to download the printer drivers on my computer. One frustrated hour later, after a slow internet connection and being unable to locate the software in any of the drawers, I shove my jump drive into Court's computer.

I don't like working from someone else's computer, but unless I want to keep digging in this box, this is my best bet.

Mrs. Stratton comes in the office. "Would you like me to make you dinner?"

I look at my watch. Six-thirty. "No. That's okay. I'll be fine."

"There are plenty of items to make a salad. Several different salad dressings in the refrigerator."

"Okay. Thanks. That sounds perfect. Have a good evening."

"Same to you. Are you almost done?"

"Getting there. I have a few more items to scan." I wave my hand over the many stacks still sitting on Court's desk.

"Should have been done long ago, in my opinion. But the Mrs. could do no wrong. In anybody's eyes. Not speaking ill of the dead, mind you, but facts are facts. I'll see you tomorrow."

With those parting words, she shuts the door.

The sound of the feeder jamming brings me back to reality.

I unjam the feeder, and restart the batch of papers.

The stack is rather large, and when it appears they will go through without jamming, I sit back at Court's desk. He only has a couple of folders on his desktop, unlike mine which is littered with documents and folders.

A cute picture of Bristol and Darling is his screensaver. As each batch finishes scanning, I hit the display button and name the file, then store it to the jump drive.

A pretty monotonous project.

Quite boring actually.

Until I accidentally hit the wrong drop down box and find myself in Court's documents folder.

There aren't too many documents. A lot less than I would expect from a business owner like Court. Unable to stop my curiosity, I scan the titles.

One catches my eye.

TAG Investigation.

What kind of investigation?

Is Court's company investigating someone or something?

Is somebody investigating Court's company?

My wandering mind is once again interrupted by the sound of the feeder jamming.

My face flushes at my nosiness.

Whatever is going on with Court's company is his business, not mine. He hired me to take care of Bristol and Darling, not snoop into his computer files and imagine crazy scenarios. Wringing information out of Jared is entirely different than opening Court's documents.

As I turn my chair to unjam the feeder I almost back into Court.

His gaze is fixed on me, his lips are in a straight line, and his arms are crossed. "Find anything interesting?"

MENACING

I'M AMAZED AT HOW calm I feel with him towering over me, looking more menacing than I know he is.

At least I hope he's not as menacing as he appears right now.

Since he hasn't moved there's nowhere for me to go. My knees are almost touching his as I continue to sit in his chair.

"Wow." I decide that honesty is the best approach. "This looks really bad, I'm sure, but I didn't open any of your documents. I accidentally hit the wrong drop down and then the printer jammed, so…"

"So I can thank the printer for keeping you out of my personal files?"

Even though his expression hasn't changed his tone is lighter.

Or maybe that's my imagination.

I want to reach up and uncross his arms.

But I don't.

That would be overstepping boundaries for sure. "I wouldn't have looked."

"And I know that because?"

"You don't. You just have to trust me."

Uncrossing his arms, he then runs a hand through his hair. His thick, black gorgeous hair.

"I've trusted you with my children, but…"

His more relaxed stance has relaxed me. "I'm telling you I didn't open anything. Please believe me."

Knowing that I didn't do anything wrong is normally all it takes for my conscious to feel okay when a situation like this comes up, but for some reason, it's important for me to know he knows I'm telling the truth.

He backs away, his gaze not leaving me. "I don't have a choice, do I?"

Those words don't settle anything inside me. They keep me on edge, a feeling I don't like.

He picks up one of the stacks that haven't been scanned. "Have you been working on this all day?"

He's not far enough around the desk that I can get to the printer, so I stay seated, which I feel puts me at a great disadvantage. I don't like looking up to him. "I have."

I decide not to reveal how interesting I find the information and in some cases, lack of information. I'm sure he knows his wife's strengths and weaknesses. We all have them.

But MaryLeigh Treyhune definitely had organizational issues.

And issues with authority, it appears.

Now I wish I had paid more attention to the television when my dad watched those races. Not that I could have gleaned much personal information from a few seconds of camera time, but it would have been interesting to see Court's interaction with MaryLeigh. If he had a smile for her, a kiss on the cheek or the lips before stepping into the race car.

Dale never would kiss me in public on the mouth. He always kissed my cheek or forehead if people were watching. I asked him about it once, and he said if he kissed me the way he did in private he might forget we were in public.

That's what he said, but he really meant that classy people didn't kiss on the mouth in public.

It wasn't a sign of status.

My parents always kissed on the lips.

Hence, no status for the Madisons.

"Why don't you call it a day?"

Court has now walked over to the door.

"I will. As soon as I unjam these papers. Then, I'm going out. I need to buy a Father's Day card for my dad. Not that's it'll get there by Father's Day."

Court stops his exit from the room. "Thanks for the reminder. I need to do the same."

Then he disappears and I open the printer once again.

"No sense in taking two cars. I'll drive."

When I look toward the door where Court's voice came from, all I see is his hand on the doorframe for a moment.

He's gone.

As I focus my attention on unjamming the printer, I realize there are far worse things in life than hanging out with Court Treyhune.

WE MAKE QUICK WORK of buying cards. Well, Court much quicker than me. I think he bought the first one he picked up, while I am more particular, reading several before finding the message I want to say to my father.

Seeing how it's June, we exit the card shop into daylight, even though it's after eight o'clock. I do notice the nice breeze that seems to never end here in the town of Hampton Cove, making it bearable to be outside.

Although, I must admit, being around Court can throw a heat-wrench into any situation. I try to stay as far away from him physically as I can.

We walk past a café with an outdoor seating area. Most of the tables are occupied, but there are a couple of empty ones.

"Are you hungry?" Court asks.

I think back to the day and the half-sandwich I had for lunch hours ago. I have no reason to lie to Court, except that he might suggest we eat together. And again, there are worse things in life. "Actually, I am. Lunch was a long time ago."

"Do you want to stop here and grab a bite?" He nods toward the café.

"Sure."

We walk to the hostess stand and in moments are literally on the other side of the fence as we are seated at a table. Now we are watching others walk by.

It's awkward sitting here with Court. I barely know him, yet am privy to many personal things about him. I notice other women looking longingly his way as they walk by. They are probably jealous of me, yet if they knew the dynamics of our relationship, they wouldn't be.

After the waiter brings our drinks, Court looks at me. "I talked to Bristol and Darling earlier. They said to tell you hello."

Bristol and Darling. Mine and Court's common denominator, Team Twin. "When you talk to them next, tell them I said hello back."

"I will."

Although he asked me on this venture, he is definitely far away in his thoughts. I wonder if he's thinking about his dad. Or the girls. Or his business.

Or maybe his dead wife.

I can see how they would all captivate his attention.

"So, you and Jared have been friends for a long time?" No harm in finding out a little background information while I can.

"You are interested." His tone and expression are flat. This is not the impression I want to give.

"Not for reasons you think." Jared and I wouldn't last a minute dating. I'd probably end up slapping him across the face, or he'd tire of being unable to impress me with his fake charms.

He scoots his chair back and crosses his right leg over his left leg. "I don't blame you. Jared is single, nice-looking, according to all the women, and he makes a decent living, although why he never has any money is beyond me. Watch out, you might have to pay for dinner if you go out with him."

I laugh. "I don't want to go out with him. Promise."

"I don't know. You are going to a concert with him. And here we are, barely settled in our seats and the first thing you do is ask about him. Sounds like you're interested."

How do I convince Court that my interest in Jared has nothing to do with the dating factor? "He's not my type. At all."

Court half smiles. "What is your type?"

"Somebody more like you." And there it is. I really said that.

I would like to say his expression looks surprised, but honestly, concerned is more of what I'm seeing on his face.

That's not good.

"Don't take it personally," I add, trying to ease his mind. "I'm talking about your whole persona. Business man. Clean cut. Handsome."

Court nods. "Jared is all those things."

"Yeah, I guess so. But there's something unreal about him. That probably doesn't make sense to you since you've known him so long."

"He's complicated, I'll admit. But he does have a good heart. I just don't think he knows that."

The sound of chairs scraping across the concrete invades the atmosphere as the table of four next to us prepare to leave. Even though it appears the two women are with the two guys, I can't help but notice the women stare at Court as they walk past us.

The guys are not staring at me.

Court demands that kind of attention.

A glimpse tells me one of them recognizes Court, but she doesn't say anything.

Court is oblivious.

I want to stop talking about Jared. I'll have to glean information on my own from now on. No more probing Court.

The door to the restaurant opens and I recognize the women who walked by a couple of minutes ago coming back toward their table. I glance over at it, thinking maybe they left something behind.

But they don't make it to their table.

No, instead they stop at ours.

"We're sorry to interrupt, but aren't you Court Treyhune?"

The woman who speaks is a platinum blonde, beautiful and expensively dressed.

Court straightens in his seat. "I am."

The blonde flushes while her friend doesn't seem affected at all. "I thought so. I just wanted to tell you I hope your dad is going to be alright. We've been praying for him."

Well, knock me down. An autograph? Yes. Slipping Court a phone number? Yes.

Telling him you've been praying for his dad? Never in a million years would I have guessed that would be the reason they sought Court out.

"Thank you."

For the first time since I've been around him, Court seems uncomfortable. His hand has settled on his knee. He has just run his other hand through his hair. And he only speaks those two words.

It's not my place to intervene.

To speak.

To do so would give these women the impression that I am somebody I'm not.

"We'll continue to pray," the blonde says. "Have a good evening."

She and her friend depart, and I wonder if they hear Court's second "thank you."

"That was nice of them." Why I feel the need to say something in their defense is beyond me.

"Prayer." Court rubs his chin with his right hand. "Interesting."

I'm given a moment to think about the exchange as the waiter takes our order. He scoops up our menus and promises to top off our waters momentarily.

He seems oblivious to who Court is.

Which is probably a relief to Court.

"I thought they were going to ask for an autograph." I might as well throw my thoughts out there.

"Me, too."

"It's good to know people are praying for you. I mean, I'm sure you know the whole racing nation is praying, but to hear personally from people, like that lady, has to be good for your soul."

His eyebrows raise. "Racing nation?"

I feel my eyes widen at my slip of "race speak." Hearing my daddy all those years has now come to life. "You know, the fans."

"Are you a fan?"

Are his eyes hopeful?

"Not really. I've never followed the sport." Which isn't a lie. Daddy followed it, I didn't.

"I like your name, by the way."

"Thank you."

He fiddles with the napkin, his gaze lingering on me. He now seems relaxed again. Like the edge the woman put on him when she mentioned prayer has now left.

Court has no faith, and he doesn't want to talk about prayer.

It's a good thing we aren't involved. That wouldn't make Mama happy at all.

MONSOON

FRIDAY MORNING BRINGS torrential rains which squash any attempt at running. Thunder rumbles early and wakens me from a night of surprisingly good sleep.

I thought the late dinner and time spent with Court might make for a restless night, but I was wrong.

Mrs. Stratton needed the day off, so I make the coffee. I've pulled my hair back in a ponytail and am reading the Wall Street Journal online when Court steps into my world.

He nods toward the back of the house where sheets of pouring rain are visible through the floor to ceiling windows.

"No outdoor activities today." He pours himself a cup of coffee before joining me at the bar.

"I agree." As I sip my coffee, I spy the card I had bought for my dad. It's addressed and stamped, ready to be mailed.

Picking it up brings fond memories of my dad. I will miss spending Father's Day with him this year.

"Need to mail that?" Court asks.

"I do. I'm sure the rain will let up soon and I'll run it out there."

Court leans over, taking the envelope out of my hand. "The mail comes first thing. I'll take it."

"No. You've already showered. I'll run it out there." I make a move to slide off my barstool, but his hand on my shoulder stops me.

"I'll do it. Keep reading."

He half-smiles and I'm mesmerized to do what he says.

Which is not like me at all.

But my gaze follows him as he walks out of the kitchen and down the hall. I hear the door open then the garage door opening.

Moments later, and I swear it's barely moments, I hear the garage door shut again.

He's back.

Like it's second nature, I jump up off the barstool when Court enters the kitchen, hair dripping and shirt speckled with large rain-soaked spots.

Grabbing a towel hanging from the oven door, I hand it to him. "Here."

He holds the thick red towel in his hand and shakes his head. "I'm not sure what Mrs. Stratton would think of me using a kitchen towel to dry my hair."

I swallow hard, waffling between not being embarrassed at my maybe lame gesture and unsure of what to say.

His expression holds a hint of mischief as he rakes the towel over his wet hair. "I guess we won't tell her."

The fact that his words have the ability to relax me doesn't escape my notice. Maybe the fact annoys me, but I'm aware.

It's impossible not to be aware of Court Treyhune on any level. "I guess we won't."

"This needs to go to the laundry room." He drapes the towel over his arm as he brushes his hair with his hands.

"Good idea. Mrs. Stratton will be none the wiser."

Once again he disappears, but I barely have time to process him leaving the room before he returns.

He doesn't stay in the kitchen. He walks into the keeping room and stands, one hand on the window, the other shoved in his pocket. The rain seems to hold his attention, and I quietly wonder if I slipped away would he even notice.

As I'm about to take a step his voice stops me.

"You're refreshingly real."

I know he's talking about me, but since I feel anything but real, an unwanted wrench settles in my stomach. He didn't ask a question, so there's no obligation to respond.

But somehow saying nothing makes his statement appear true.

Isn't that what I want?

"Bristol and Darling are real, but they're only ten," he continues, his gaze still focused on the monsoon falling outside. "Other than them, I'm surrounded by people who are who they think I want them to be." Now he turns to me. "Why do you think that is?"

Even with his rain-splattered shirt and wet hair, he makes a perfectly contrasted backdrop to the gray skies and falling rain. It's almost like he's too beautiful to be real, but he is real.

And he's accusing his friends of not being real.

"I'm not qualified to answer that."

Stepping away from the window he walks toward me. All of him, moving at a slow pace, giving me time to dwell on every step he takes.

Every inch of space that closes between us causes my heart to do strange things.

Like hope.

And beat faster at that hope.

The hope that one day I will love again.

He stops dangerously close to me.

Dangerous because we've only known each other a short time, yet he seems unbothered by the closeness.

Maybe he's unaware?

No. His gaze says he's not. Dark eyes in which the wall that was there at our first meeting seems to have had a brick or two knocked out of it. Like a sliver of light has entered into his eyes.

My face heats as he reaches out and tucks a strand of hair that has escaped my ponytail behind my ear.

"Thank you, Shelby. Thank you for being real and reminding me what's important."

The heat from my face quickly fades as the icy truth runs through me.

He has no idea who I am.

"DO YOU MIND IF I share this space with you?"

I look up from the files I'm looking through in Court's office as I hear his voice. "No. It's your office. Your meeting must have gone well if you are home early."

My imposter self is sitting on the settee with my laptop on my lap and the papers, now in file folders, sitting on the coffee table.

Court walks around his desk and settles in his chair. "It did. Thanks."

After a few moments, I realize I can sit here all day watching him work. That part of me is real.

Honest.

Maybe that's what he's picking up on. My realness toward him, because everything else about me is like those people he described that he surrounds himself with.

I wonder if he puts Jared in that category as well.

I would, but I haven't been around long.

Still, there is a decisive fakeness I detect from Jared.

As I peruse the homeschool files, Court is busy working on his computer. After a few minutes, the printer starts, and I realize I've done more Court-gazing than perusing of the homeschool information in front of me.

Court's cell phone rings, startling me. From his side of the conversation I learn the call is from his assistant, Susan. He asks her to hold on for a minute.

He turns to me. "I need to take this in the other room. Can you make sure these pages print okay? Sometimes if the output bin gets too full, they fall on the floor."

"Sure."

He nods his head and leaves the room, shutting the door behind him.

His conversation with Susan must be very private.

The sound of the printer jamming brings back memories of when I was trying to scan yesterday.

I set my laptop on the coffee table, lay the papers that have already printed on Court's desk, and proceed to unjam the printer.

He's printing on legal size paper, and the tray is empty.

I scour the credenza and finally find a ream of legal paper, so I load the printer and push the start button.

What looks to be a financial statement is printing, but when that finishes, copies of checks start printing.

Finding a paper clip on his desk, I clip the financial statement together, then deciding that wasting legal paper isn't smart, I switch the paper back to letter size.

I see the checks are all made out to one vendor. Rajed Media. The checks are pretty hefty amounts.

Looking at the still-closed door, I perch on the edge of Court's chair and pick up the financial statement.

Thankful for my financial background, I quickly find the account that is listed on the check.

Prepaid account.

Of course.

The printer quiets indicating it's finished printing and I reach over and grab the rest of the papers.

All of which are still copies of the checks to Rajed Media. As I stack the checks, I realize the last check doesn't have the same account number listed as the first couple of checks that printed.

No, this is another account, still a liability account, but this is an expense account.

Flipping to the expense page of the financial statement, I see the last check is cut to an expense account while some of the other checks are cut out of a prepaid account.

Strange.

Normally vendors who are set up as prepaid aren't paid out of the expense. That might mean the expense is being charged twice. Especially if it is the same invoice.

I flip through the checks and find four more that are charged to the expense account. But there are no invoice numbers on the checks to reference back to.

Maybe that's why Court is printing them. He knows something doesn't look right.

A clicking sound turns my attention to the door knob, which I see turning, and I realize Court is coming back.

I scoot a away from the desk, acting like I'm straightening the stack.

He shoves his phone back into the case that is clipped to his belt and I can tell by his motions that the phone call wasn't pleasant.

"Thank you for monitoring the printer." His tone is clipped like he's not thankful at all, but I'm not taking it personally.

Because he's real.

And that's much better than putting on an act.

Even if the act is truly how you want to be.

I stand and step back toward the window as he comes around. His agitated state doesn't hinder the manly scent that surrounds him. I hope he doesn't become more agitated that I changed the paper.

He picks up the stack of check copies as I scoot around and make my way back to the safety of the settee.

Leaning back in his chair, he flips the copies of the checks just like I did a few minutes ago. His expression doesn't change, which means he's not giving me any indication of his understanding of what he is reading.

He clips the check copies to the financial statement.

The gray of the day has crept into the room, into the atmosphere. In fact, it might be stormier in here than it is outside at the moment.

Court stands and lays the papers on his desk. "I need you to come with me."

It must be my crazed expression that has him add a "please" to his request.

"Please? I'll explain in the car."

"Okay."

Closing my laptop, I follow him out of the office.

Within minutes we are heading down the main road of the subdivision, neither of us saying a word.

As we turn right out of the subdivision, I see a car that looks like Jared's pulling into the subdivision.

"Hey, isn't that—"

Court guns the engine as he turns right, and I hesitate before finishing my question.

I point my thumb toward the back of Court's SUV. "That looked like Jared's car."

"It was."

Court's answer makes it more than clear why we are leaving his house. The empty roadway in front of us apparently gives him the license to drive fast, but then he mutters something about the rain and slows his speed to a respectable pace.

All of these driving skills have me questioning why he doesn't drive on the racetrack.

My other question?

Why are we avoiding Jared?

WE PULL INTO AN almost empty parking lot by the water. Rain is still misting as gray skies hover. All of which appear to match Court's mood. We sit in silence in the parking lot for a minute, the SUV still running, cranking out the cold air that is fogging the windows.

Or maybe it's the heat from Court's anger.

Or whatever emotion it is that has us acting like runaways.

Runaways from our own home.

Even though it's only my temporary home, it's still my home.

"You probably think I'm crazy."

His voice slices through the frosty air, not really demanding an answer, but not rejecting one either.

"Not crazy. Just bothered by something."

His hands still grasp the steering wheel. It's as if letting go would indicate he was ready to let go of whatever emotion is driving him.

No pun intended.

But something has to give and I'm not sure he even knows what that something is. "Do you want to get out? Walk around a bit? The air might do us some good."

I say us like this is our problem.

"It's still raining," he says, his grip still tight on the wheel.

"I won't melt. And neither will you. You proved that this morning."

His knuckles shift slightly, like he might be considering my suggestion. His right hand pushes the button that turns off the engine. "Come on."

We exit his ride, the air thick with humidity. He shoves his hands in his pocket and it's only then I realize he's still in dress clothes.

Expensive dress clothes I'm sure.

My jeans and blouse will recover from the wet.

I hope his clothes do the same.

They're probably dry clean only.

His dress shoes look like they are in a foreign country as they traipse over the wet gravel lot. Specks of wet gravel dust quickly splatter across the black shine, but I doubt he even notices.

I wonder why I do.

Because I'm doing everything I can to keep from looking at his face. Looking into maybe more bricks being pushed out of the walls that are his eyes.

The more his eyes reveal, the more I become drawn into who he is and what his hurts are.

It's evident to me Court is a man of hurts.

"It's complicated."

I know he's talking to himself as well as to me. "I'm sure."

"You're so very different from her."

I almost misstep as I walk. Me? This emotional upheaval he's dealing with has to do with me?

Impossible.

We step onto a boardwalk. An almost deserted boardwalk. There are a couple of people hanging in the mist like we are. The wind is blowing, providing relief from the thick air, and I'm glad I have my hair pulled back.

Benches to our left beg to be sat on, but their seats, damp from the rain, stop any thoughts of sitting. Court's dress shoes thump against the wood of the boardwalk, probably a sound not heard much here.

"When MaryLeigh died, I thought that was it for that part of my life. I didn't want to marry again, didn't want to fall in love again. I thought Bristol, Darling and I would have a great life together. Just us three."

Now I wish I had something to hold onto. "You guys do have a great life together, don't you?" *Did he say fall in love?*

"I don't know about it being great. I know I work a lot. I know the girls miss me, because I miss them."

"You are running three businesses. It is three, isn't it?"

He nods. "Yeah. Three."

"That's not easy. Don't be too hard on yourself. I'm sure the girls understand."

"How can they when I barely understand it?"

At least we have left talking about his love life. Or the promise of him never having another one. Whew. That was a scary topic there for a minute. "On some level they know you have to work. Money doesn't grow on trees."

The breeze continues to blow, making his shirt ripple, accentuating his abs.

Now that I've seen them with my own eyes, I have no trouble imagining what's inside his shirt.

"That call I received? It was from Susan."

"Susan your secretary?" Dale had a secretary.

Dale.

I haven't thought about him in a while.

Could it be? Am I healing from his crazy words which brought me heartbreak?

"She called to tell me Jared was on his way over."

"So why did we have to leave?"

His expression looks pained at this point. So much so that I blurt out, "You don't have to tell me. I'm being nosy."

Scents of fried food from the faithful vendors mingles with the mist and Court's angst as our steps slow. Court stops then turns to me.

"Jared has always wanted everything I have. And now it seems he wants my nanny."

MINISTRY

"WHAT?" THIS MIST has turned into a light sprinkle, and I wipe my eyes.

"Susan said he spent half the time he was at work today singing your praises and talking about how beautiful you are and bragged how quickly he landed a date with you."

"It's not a date."

"Perception is everything." His tone is matter of fact.

And he's right. I didn't think or care how Jared viewed my acceptance. I might have to unaccept.

That would be awkward.

Awkward like standing here in the rain with Court.

"I'll tell him I can't go. I don't want this to interfere with my job or the man who hired me." I smile as I say this last part, even though I still don't understand why Jared talking me up to Susan would cause such a reaction in Court.

Unless it's a pattern Court is tired of. I decide to find out. "Do you always feel like you're having to defend what's yours? Not that I'm yours. Geez. That came out all wrong." I turn away from him and slowly start walking back toward his SUV.

"Shelby, wait."

The way he says my name makes me like my name. Or maybe I just like my name said with all the angst that's brewing inside Court. But I do as he says.

I wait.

It's only moments before he's next to me. His face searches mine. "This is crazy, isn't it? Us standing here in the rain like this?"

I laugh. "It is."

"The Jared thing. I'm used to it. I'm used to him. What I'm not used to is the way I feel right now."

"Meaning?"

"Jealous. For the first time in a long time, I feel jealous."

Court's revelation heats my face.

"I know, it's crazy. You think I'm crazy."

"I don't know what to think."

"Think on this. Let's have dinner."

I want to ask him if *he's* asking me on a date, but I don't dare. Date? Confession time? I'm confused.

But I'm there. "Okay."

I'VE SHOWERED, MY hair is in big curlers that I brought on a whim and I'm standing in front of my closet wishing I had brought other clothes on a whim.

Bristol's words play through my mind. *That's ugly.*

The ten-year-old was right and has impeccable taste in clothing, I'm now thinking.

Fun. What did I bring that is fun?

Then I pull a cease-fire on all these thoughts. This whole dinner thing is crazy anyway. Court probably asked me to dinner simply to make Jared angry.

Great.

I've come six-hundred-plus miles to escape heartbreak only to become a pawn in a power struggle between two best friends.

In a move that I know is defiant, I pull out a plain black blouse and a gray pair of slacks. Pulling everything on and buttoning everything up I look in the mirror.

Perfect.

Absolutely nothing sexy or flirty with this outfit.

I pull the curlers out of my hair, embarrassed that I even put them in to begin with. Brushing as hard as I can, I finally put my hair up in a bun when I realize a couple of strands have escaped, proof that the curls refuse to be totally tamed.

Pawn indeed.

Slipping my feet into black ballet flats, I think about toning down my makeup, but the clock reveals I don't have time.

I gaze into the full-length mirror, satisfied with my attire and look. If Court was looking for a sexy date to make Jared mad, he's going to be disappointed.

If he asked me out for me, well, this is who I am.

Or rather, who the world thinks I am.

COURT ISN'T IN the kitchen. I look into the living room, and he's not there either.

Glancing at my phone I see it's six o'clock. The time he said we would leave. My soft-soled shoes don't make any noise as I walk to the office. The door is open, so I peek in. Court is staring at his desk with a perplexed expression on his face.

He's holding the stack of papers he had printed earlier.

"Everything okay?" I ask.

Setting the papers down on the desk, he starts toward the door. "Yes. I thought I remembered leaving the papers on the left side of the desk, but I guess not."

I can tell he's talking more to himself than he is to me, but that doesn't stop me from responding. "You did. They were right by your mouse."

"That's what I thought. But when I came in here just now they were sitting here."

He points to where the papers are sitting.

"That's weird." It's then I notice Court's attire. He's in a beige, loose button-up shirt, that's got a wrinkled-on-purpose look, brown shorts, and brown slip-on shoes.

Totally casual.

And as I'm checking out his sportswear, he's checking out my non-sportswear.

Tilting his head to the right with a glimpse of his smile emerging, he nods. "I like the outfit. Very classy. But since the weather has pushed out, I thought we might have dinner on the boat. My bad. Sorry I didn't mention that when I asked. If that's not to your liking we can do something else."

I run my hand down my slack-clad leg. "No. Dinner on a boat sounds fun. I'll, uh, I'll go change. Be right back."

Quickly scanning my wardrobe through my mind, I'm wondering what I brought that would work for this dinner. I did bring a couple of pair of shorts, so I pull them out. I slip on the denim pair and a white tank top, then pull on a long-sleeved white sheer cover up. I also kick off the ballet flats to slip my feet into a worn pair of flip-flops.

As I start to walk out of the room, I spy my sunglasses on the dresser. Definitely will need these now that the sun is out. I take my hair out of its bun, and run my fingers through the loose waves. I push my sunglasses on like a headband and glance in the mirror.

Ready.

Court is waiting for me as I enter the kitchen.

"Much better boat-wear. You also look more comfortable."

I do feel more comfortable, but he's not supposed to notice that. Why does Court pick up on vibes I don't want to give out? "How can one not be comfortable in slouchy clothes?"

"Slouchy? I like that word. Come on, slouch."

I follow him to his SUV wondering what I'm really doing.

WHEN HE SAID dinner on a boat, he meant dinner on a boat. I thought casual dinner cruise or something along those lines. But no, we picked up dinner from a local grocer, and we are on his boat.

It's more like a yacht. Small yacht if there is such a thing.

But we aren't going anywhere.

We are going to sit in his boat, in the slip.

This seems to be the thing to do on a Friday night in Hampton Cove.

The marina is about a ten-minute drive from the grocery store. After parking his SUV, he takes a picnic basket out of the back. We each carry a couple of bags of food, and I follow him as we make our way down the wooden dock to his boat.

He nods to a couple of people as we walk. By the surprised looks on their faces, I wonder how long it's been since he's done this.

Or who he has done this with last.

Music drifts from different boats, from classic rock songs to classical instrumentals. White party lights drape across some of the bigger boats.

Strands of untamed hair keep flying in my face, bringing images of

Bristol and Darling to mind.

We sit on the top level of the boat. The view is amazing, enabling us to see everything from the endless water to the other boats. Court's shirt billows as he pulls out two wine glasses from the picnic basket. He digs through a compartment and comes up with a corkscrew.

"One glass of Pinot Noir coming up."

He hands me the glasses as he uncorks the wine. Unceremoniously, he pours the wine, then sets the bottle in a wine bucket.

He holds his glass up in a toasting position, and I follow suit. As our glasses touch I can't help notice a haunted look in his eyes. The still-bright sky, summer breeze, and bay-water scent can't erase the sadness that this man has inside of him.

"To a night of forgetting everything but the here and now," he toasts.

Our gaze doesn't break as we each sip our wine. In as much as I'm reading what he's feeling, I wonder what, if anything, he thinks about me? Can he see, through my eyes, the war raging inside of me?

Frankly, I'm tired of my inner battle. Tired of thinking about heartbreak and losing the life I'd known for so long. What could be the harm in letting it all go for one evening?

One evening with a guy who doesn't know anything about me, really. Who isn't pressuring me to live up to standards he has set for his life. The toast he made is like a balm to my heart. Maybe I can forget for one evening.

It's certainly worth a try.

I settle onto the bench seat. "This is nice. I've never had dinner on a boat, in a slip at a dock."

"As you can see, Friday nights are hopping at the marina. I bring the girls out here sometimes. They love it. Although they do get restless quickly. It's a fast dinner night when they are here."

I laugh. "I can imagine."

I also imagine their hair flying all over the place. I'm sure Crystal has tamed that beast by now.

Having put our food into a cooler, Court joins me on the seat. There's plenty of room for more than two people, but he chooses to sit closer to me, rather than farther away. His knee almost brushes mine, and I try not to think about his body touching mine.

This dinner seems too intimate for a man trying to make his friend mad. It also seems too intimate for a man who doesn't know a woman very well. How about too intimate for a man who's still mourning the loss of his wife?

I'm not sure what I will say if he starts in about how he and MaryLeigh used to come here. Maybe he doesn't have anyone to talk to about his loss?

"I don't take this boat out nearly enough." Court taps the back of the boat.

"What's stopping you? Time?"

He twirls his wine glass between his thumb and forefinger. "Time, memories, any number of things."

"I understand."

"Maybe fear."

Surprised by his admission, I take a sip of the wine. "Fear? What could you be afraid of?"

"You say *you* like I'm a different species from the rest of the world."

I place my hand on my forehead. "You know what I mean."

"This thing with my dad scared me. Jolted me back to life, in a way."

"Back to life?"

"It's like nothing mattered to me for a long time. And that's not good. It's like I was afraid of living. Really living."

For a long time translates into when MaryLeigh died. I know this. "Sometimes we need a kick-start."

He looks at me. "Did you need a kick-start? Is that why you came south, on a whim, at the last minute, to be a nanny, something which you had never done before?"

The fading sun seems much warmer now that it had a few minutes ago. I brush my blowing hair away from my eyes, grateful for the respite it gives me before answering. "If I'm honest, yes."

"Funny, isn't it, how things work out. Here we are, sitting on this boat, you and me, strangers except for some professional knowledge we have of each other, yet to me, this feels natural. Not strained or trying in any way."

"Like we don't have to put on airs, pretend we're feeling one way when we're not. Pretend we're somebody we're not." I hope I say the words convincingly as I sip my wine.

"You have no expectations of me."

"Except to give me a paycheck."

He wants to smile, I can tell, but it doesn't quite happen. He does continue to look at me though.

Searching.

His eyes are still guarded, but softer.

"Neighbor! Hi."

Court and I both look toward the dock. I see the guy that nodded to me as I was running. He's holding hands with a smiling blonde woman, who despite a scar running across her cheek, is one of the most beautiful women I have ever seen.

"Stephen, isn't it?" Court says.

"It is. And this is my wife, Jenny."

"Nice to meet you." Jenny's gaze focuses on me.

Court catches on. "This is Shelby. My children's nanny."

"Hi," I say as both Stephen and Jenny smile like he's telling the biggest lie ever. And I can't blame them for thinking he's lying. I'm draped across the bench seat of this boat, wine glass in hand.

Working hard for the money, as the song goes. "Nice to meet you." I nod toward Stephen. "I saw you running the other morning."

He nods, recognition on his face. "Yes. The running junkies get out early."

"Not early enough," I say. "I started leaving an hour earlier. This heat is brutal."

"I guess I'm used to it."

Stephen's thumb brushes Jenny's hand as he speaks. She's simply radiant and beautiful and lovely looking.

Even with that scar.

Must be nice.

But I can tell, looking at her and Stephen, that it comes from within. That the beauty I'm seeing isn't necessarily about the way they're put together physically, although they are put together beautifully in a way a lot of people wished they were put together.

With the momentary silence, the atmosphere becomes awkward.

"Would you care to join us?" Court asks.

"I wish we could, but we have some friends expecting us." Stephen points further down the dock.

Jenny looks my way. "You should bring the girls over. Our housekeeper, Teresa, has a nine-year-old girl, Phoebe. I know she would love some company. Especially now that school's out."

"I'll do that. Maybe next week." Anything to keep the girls busy sounds like a good plan to me.

"Also," Stephen says. "I know my uncle Roger has been over to your place a couple of times. We are still having church in my house. We'd love to have you. We have a great ministry started. There are quite a number of kids coming. Your girls might like it. And it's close to home."

I sense the atmosphere around Court has tensed.

Stifled.

Shifted.

He takes a long sip of his wine. Probably trying to think of a polite way to refuse the beautiful couple's offer of attending church.

At their house, no less.

I've heard of people doing that but have never personally known any house church people.

"We'll think about it," Court says. "Thank you for the invitation."

"All right. I'm glad we ran into you." Stephen takes a step back. "Nice meeting you, Shelby. We hope we see you guys soon."

"Bye," Jenny says.

Court and I say goodbye and settle back on the bench seat as they walk down the dock.

"So now you've met your neighbors."

"I've actually met Stephen once before. There was a wedding going on in the cul-de-sac, and Bristol and Darling decided to have a fight in the street. In the middle of the wedding. It wasn't the best of days. Stephen met me in the street to see if he could be of any help."

"How cool to have a wedding at that gazebo. Who got married?"

Court stretches his arm across the back of the seat, his fingertips dangerously close to my shoulder. They could touch me if they wanted to. I want them to.

"The people who live across the cul-de-sac from me, but I don't know them."

Court's voice reels me back to the fact that he is talking and we are having a conversation. I need to participate. "Sounds to me like you need to get to know your neighbors. They seem to have a lot of fun."

"I'm usually working." He takes a sip of his wine.

"Maybe we can change that."

"Maybe." His fingers touch the back of my shoulder. "I like the way you say we."

The scent of the water, the feel of his hand, the romantic atmosphere.

Court's words.

All of those things combine to make this seem like a real date. Not a date to make one's best friend jealous. Not a date to kill time because there is nothing better to do.

If this is what happens when you forget the here and now, I might lose my whole memory bank.

MANSION

SATURDAY MORNING WE land in North Carolina in a much tamer fashion than when we had made our trip at the beginning of the week. Apparently, news of Cal's recovery has squelched the intense media scrutiny, and no one approaches us as we exit the plane and make our way to the waiting car.

We're silent as Court drives. I replay last night's dinner through my mind. A real date normally ends with a kiss.

And ours didn't.

So I'm not sure what to call what happened and didn't happen last night. Maybe it was a night of simply relaxing. Nothing more.

Nothing less.

"Ready to get back to work?" Court asks as we drive down a long driveway.

"Sure. It's what you pay me for, right?"

He doesn't answer, but that's okay, because I'm too busy focusing on the house that comes into view.

And I thought Court's house was big.

It has nothing on this gorgeous mansion nestled in the midst of rolling green hills. Perfectly manicured, sculpted and colorful, the landscape has me at a loss for words. "This is where your mom and dad live?"

"This is Casa de Treyhune."

I glance over at Court, knowing in that moment that he will never, ever, ever see where my parents live.

Ever.

Although my mom is a neat freak, and my dad takes pride in his yard, which consists of a patch of grass surrounding the trailer, there's a level of discomfort that settles in my soul regarding the home I grew up in.

And yes, it is a home in every sense of the word. Clean, loving, gracious.

Full of Jesus.

But those things didn't seem important to the other kids at school. The kids who lived in the big houses turned their noses up at kids like me.

Until Paul took notice of me.

Then when Paul unnoticed me, after I gave him the most precious gift I could give a boy, I was once again the recipient of upturned noses and snobbish behavior.

I learned early on it's who you are in life that matters.

And what you have establishes who you are.

We park the car and barely have the doors open when Bristol and Darling come running out to meet us.

Court rather.

I stand to the side and watch the girls' amazing affection for their father, who hugs them in return.

"Daddy, we're so glad you're back. We missed you. Grandpa Cal is here. He came home yesterday."

As they are all wrapped in their hug I look closer at the girls, not believing what I'm seeing.

Their hair.

It's still a mess.

Tangled, wrangled and hanging down their backs. They keep pushing it out of their faces.

Oh well, who am I to judge? They were around me for over twenty-four hours and I honestly had no time to take a brush to it.

With Cal's return and the time needed to prepare for that, Vera and Crystal probably have been busy doing other things.

More important things than worrying about two girls who are happy with things the way they are.

Maybe that's the issue.

Why fix what's not broke?

At Court's prompt, the girls come over and give me a hug.

"Have you been having fun?" I ask.

"Yes! And we're going to have a party!"

They are jumping up and down, and it's then I notice they are still wearing their bands on their wrists. "Party?"

"For Father's Day. Daddy, we made you a present." Bristol smiles big as she speaks.

Darling pulls Bristol's sleeve. "You weren't supposed to tell him, Bristol. It was supposed to be a surprise."

Crossing her arms, Darling's lower lip can't stick out much further.

Do these girls always fight?

"It's okay, Darling. Whatever it is will still be a surprise. Let's go inside. I want to see Grandpa Cal."

My knees are shaky as we walk toward the house and in the door. We enter from the garage into the biggest kitchen I've ever seen in my life. It sparkles and shines and boasts the newest and best appliances. Yet it doesn't feel uncomfortable.

It brings memories of my parents' home to my mind, which is crazy. My parents' trailer could almost fit in this kitchen alone.

I can hear the buzz of conversation not far away. We continue walking and enter a great room where a crowd is gathered. I should have known by the amount of cars outside that there were plenty of people here, but somehow, around Court, I'm not always thinking straight.

I tend to be thinking about him and how attractive he is, and how I'm so much not like him, that the realities of my surroundings don't come into focus until much later.

Like now.

Slowly everyone realizes we are here. I see Crystal and her twins. Storm couldn't hide in a crowd even if he wanted to.

I notice Davey sitting away from everyone on the hearth of a stacked stone fireplace that reaches all the way to the top of the cathedral ceiling. Everyone starts backing away from the circle they have made.

The circle around Cal Treyhune.

My breath hitches as I realize I'm about to meet one of racing's greatest, and guilt assails me at how my father would love to be in this moment. Me, not so much.

Yet here I am.

I hang back as Court approaches his father.

Greetings of hello and hugs all serenade Court as he makes his way to Cal. Vera stays close by Cal's side, her arm never leaving his shoulder, and the look of love never leaving her face.

"Dad. You have no idea how good it is to see you."

Court leans over and hugs his father, whose eyes tear up when he sees his son.

"Good to see you, Court."

Their exchange makes me ache for my father. For the hugs he gives me.

For the love he gives me.

In moments the silent crowd is silent no more. Conversation reigns and I have trouble deciding where to focus my interest.

Bristol and Darling are chatting with Taylor and Saylor. Davey is focused on his tablet.

Crystal makes her way to me. "Hi, Shelby. Don't let this crowd overwhelm you. They wouldn't hurt a fly."

"Is it that obvious?"

She laughs. "Yes. But like I said, we're harmless. And there will be even more of us tomorrow. This is what we call breaking you in gently."

"Thanks for that." In as many people are gathered, my gaze keeps drifting to Court. Whoever was sitting in the chair closest to Cal gave it up, and Court is sitting there now. He and his father seem to have a lot to talk about, while Vera's gaze scans her living room.

But she doesn't leave Cal's side.

"Are you guys leaving tomorrow night?" Crystal asks.

"That's the plan. I only packed for one night per Court's instructions."

"Maybe the girls and I can come down for a visit this summer. Taylor and Saylor really miss Court's girls. They spent so much time together until Court whisked them all away to Florida. I don't want them to lose that bond, you know?"

Yes, I know that bond. Or rather, I know what it's like not to have that bond. "Yeah. That would be great. I'm sure the girls would love to have company."

My thoughts drift to the conversation we had with Stephen and Jenny regarding their housekeeper's daughter, Phoebe. I need to remember that and ask the girls if they would be interested in meeting her.

"I'm worried about Vera." Crystal shrugs in the direction of the couple. "I can't imagine what she's been through with this scare regarding Cal, but she's not acting like herself. She won't leave his side for a minute.

She rejected all the nurses who might have come here for aftercare. In a minute she'll probably take him back to their room to rest. She's not been letting him visit with anyone too long. I'm surprised the celebration is still on for tomorrow."

As if she heard Crystal, Vera announces to Court that his father needs to rest. Court helps his dad up, and Cal waves at everyone, telling them he'll see them in a little while.

All eyes stay on the Vera and Cal.

All eyes but Court's.

His are on me.

"Dad, wait. I'd like you to meet somebody."

Court closes the space between us with the whole family watching. It's so quiet, like we're in our own world. How his expression indicates that we have a world that's our own, I'll never know, but it does. "I'd like you to meet my dad."

"Sure." I try to focus on how my dad would react at meeting his hero because that pushes away thoughts of why Court wants to introduce me to his dad.

When we reach Vera and Court, Vera hugs me. "Nice to see you again. I was so focused on Cal I didn't notice you."

"Not notice her?" Cal's voice is strong, much stronger than his appearance reveals. "She's too pretty not to notice. Hello, there."

He holds his hand out, and I take it. His grip is strong like his voice, and I'm thinking Vera is being very cautious in her care.

"Hi."

"Dad, this is Shelby."

Cal smiles and it reaches all the way to the time-wrinkled skin around his eyes. "Shelby, huh? Damn good name. I like it."

"Cal?" Vera's admonishment is all in how she says his name.

Cal shakes his head. "Sorry. Not supposed to talk like that. Especially in front of ladies and kids. Darn good name."

"Thank you."

Vera starts to steer Cal away. "Proof he needs to rest. He's forgetting his manners. See y'all at dinner."

I step back to allow Cal to walk in front of me, and find myself leaning into Court's chest. The warmth is inviting, but I cannot impose. As I attempt to slide past him, I stumble, and Court places his hands on my shoulders, holding me against him while we watch, along with the others, Cal and Vera walk out of the living room.

The touch of Court's fingers, and the fact that he didn't introduce me as his children's nanny, have me wondering what is going through Court's mind.

THE BIG HOUSE echoes the silence of the night as I stand in the kitchen drinking a glass of water while Court settles the girls in bed.

After an afternoon of a host of outdoor games, the Treyhune clan cleaned up for a massive dinner. The guys cooked on the grill while the women made a slew of cold salads and iced tea sweet enough to cause several cavities. Now, everyone has gone, leaving only Court, Team Twin and myself to stay at Cal and Vera's house. Even though the place is huge, I can't help but feel comfortable in it as I see family pictures everywhere. Knickknacks the kids have made for their grandma and grandpa are displayed proudly on tables as if they were high-dollar art pieces.

No one tiptoes around this place. The kids barrel through the halls and staircases like they are at an amusement park.

Life is lived here.

It's not a façade.

"I hope we didn't overwhelm you today."

Vera's voice startles me.

She opens the refrigerator and pours herself a glass of milk.

"No. Everyone is so nice."

"It's easy to be nice to someone who is nice in return. Everyone likes you."

She sits at the breakfast area table, and it seems like it would be rude for me to walk away. Yet, maybe she wants to be alone and it would be rude for me to stay.

"Sit."

Her sweet voice settles my dilemma, and grabbing my glass I join her.

I can tell this thing with Cal is tiring her as her eyes don't have the same life to them as they did last week when I first met her. It looks like she's dropped some weight as well, weight she couldn't afford to lose.

"So, tell me. Are you more than the nanny?"

My face heats at her question. "No."

"Damn, I mean darn."

We both laugh at her intentional way of bringing humor into the room.

"I want to see my son happy and sharing his life with someone. Someone who truly loves him. This thing with Cal proves how we must live every day to its fullest potential."

"I'm sure Court will meet someone eventually."

She keeps one hand around her glass, the other taps the side of it like she's playing a piano. "I don't know what's wrong with you? You're an intelligent, pretty gal. Good with the girls. What more could he want?"

Somebody he loves and who loves him back is what I'm thinking.

She pats the top of my hand. "It's okay. It's a rhetorical question. I can see your wheels spinning trying to think of an answer that won't encourage or offend me."

"It's just—"

"I know," she interrupts. "I'm tired and overthinking everything. I probably should catch some sleep while Cal is. The problem is my mind stays awake, reliving everything that has happened."

I point to her glass. "Maybe you can warm your milk. I've heard that will make you sleep."

Vera grimaces, still managing to look beautiful. "Tried that last night. Tasted awful and didn't work."

"I'm not a fan either." I don't tell her I can sympathize with her inability to sleep. Lately, my sleep has been very broken.

Like my life.

"Well," Vera says as she stands. "I'm going to give it the old college try. I'll see you tomorrow. Goodnight."

"Goodnight. I'll take that." I nod toward her glass.

"Thank you." She takes my hands in hers and for a moment I wonder what she is going to say.

But she doesn't say anything. I notice the hopeful look in her eyes before she leaves.

Shaking my head, I walk to the sink and set our glasses in it.

Flipping lights out as I walk, I let the moonlight guide my path.

Shadows of darkness cause me to stumble as I reach the stairs.

"Easy. I have you."

And indeed he does. Court's hands are on either side of my hips, steadying me. "Thanks."

"Sorry. I've been sitting here thinking. I just saw Mom walk back to her bedroom. I didn't realize you were still up."

"I came down for a drink of water."

He scoots over on the step. "Want to sit for a minute?"

"Sure." As I speak the word, it comes to me that the steps aren't very wide, and once again, I will be extremely close to this man whose touch takes me places I'm not ready to go.

"Welcome to my thinking place."

Our legs brush as I sit on the stairs. I would surmise that I should be becoming used to the feel of him, but I'm pretty sure his touch is something I will never become used to.

"When I was a kid, I would sit here if I had a problem."

"Did it help?" I ask.

"Not always. But it always gave me a good sense of direction. Up or down. I considered going back to my room upstairs a means of looking up, or going up. Moving forward. Sounds stupid, but it worked for me."

"It doesn't sound stupid. And like you said, if it worked…"

"Did you have a favorite thinking spot?"

Memories tumble through my mind. Memories I've suppressed far too long to reveal now.

Especially to someone like Court Treyhune. His family's fortune is probably one of the biggest around.

I've been burned by his kind in the worst way, and I vowed I wouldn't put myself in that position ever again.

But for the first time since I made that vow as a hurt seventeen-year-old, I find myself drawn once again to the mystery of a man that is way out of my league.

Maybe Court is different.

Maybe he wouldn't care about my background.

My upbringing.

Maybe if I told him my favorite thinking spot was sitting on the steps going up to my trailer, he wouldn't think twice about it.

I can't believe my mind is actually going to that place. That place of revealing my past.

But Court speaks, squelching any words that might have come out of my mouth.

"MaryLeigh and Jared grew up together."

MINGLING

HIS WORDS ARE like a confession, only I don't see what he has to confess. His tone indicates it's a fact that doesn't set well with him. "They did?"

"Yes. Only I didn't find out until after I married MaryLeigh. Not that it would have mattered, but the fact that they kept it hidden mattered."

"Kept it hidden? When did you find out?"

"About a year before she became sick. We were all out together and someone from their past saw us, came over and started talking about the old days."

"Awkward."

"Very."

The rooms are dark, but the floor-length windows let in moonlight which casts shadows across the floor. I wonder what it is about the darkness that turns Court into someone who wants to reveal things.

It's like the darkness is a catalyst for emptying his heart. "What was their reason for keeping this from you?"

"I'm not sure. I've learned that the truth and MaryLeigh and Jared don't always line up. I'm still trying to mesh it all together."

"Oh." My heart flutters for a moment. I tell myself I'm not lying to Court. So what if there are things about me he doesn't know? I'm the nanny for his children.

Not someone he's interested in spending his future with. "I liked to sit on the steps, too." No need to reveal any details about the steps.

Where they led.

The fact that they were weathered and wooden, not covered in plush carpet.

Steps are steps.

"I'm comfortable around you. I'm not comfortable around a lot of people."

I don't know whether to say thank you or not.

And he makes comfortable sound like a favorite, worn shirt. Like comfortable is something he's resigned himself to, not something he's looking forward to.

I want to be what somebody is looking forward to.

I stand, the urgent need to end this conversation overwhelming me. This, he and I, will never work, so why I'm sitting here reminiscing about his past, refusing to reveal mine is beyond me. "Goodnight."

Carefully I turn, making my way up the stairs quickly before he can say anything that will change my mind.

FATHER'S DAY DAWNS sunny and warm. I want to call my dad early, before the festivities begin. I'm sure the day will fly by and we have to be at the airport at four o'clock to go back to Florida.

I tiptoe through the house, not wanting to wake anyone. Crystal is in the kitchen, but her nose is buried in her coffee and newspaper simultaneously, and she doesn't even acknowledge that I pass by.

I find a spot outside where my cell service is excellent and call my dad.

"Happy Father's Day to the best dad in the world." I hope my tone sounds lighthearted and fun, not worried and secretive.

"Shelbs. How's my favorite girl?"

I laugh. "Mom must be at church. She thinks she's your favorite girl."

"You're both my favorite girls." In my mind I can see him smile, which makes me miss him that much more. Except for a summer or two where I was at camp, I've always spent Father's Day with my dad.

Oh, and last year. I ditched my dad in favor of Dale's dad. "I miss you, Dad. Especially today. Of course I mailed my card late. It should arrive on Monday."

"Ah, honey. You know I don't need a card. Just hearing your voice is all I need. Florida treating you okay?"

"It is." The least possible said is the best in this situation.

"Good. Your mama and I are trying hard not to be worried about you with the break up and all that. Trying real hard. You sure you're doing all right?"

"I am. I promise." Again, short and sweet.

"I'll take your word for it. What part of Florida are you in? I don't think your mama told me."

Mama didn't tell you because I didn't tell her. To blow off the question would draw more attention than telling them. "Kind of between Orlando and Miami. It's a little town. You probably haven't heard of it. Hampton Cove."

"Hampton Cove? What do you mean I probably haven't heard of it? That's where Court Treyhune lives. Cal Treyhune's son. He owns all those car dealerships in those parts."

"Oh." To say anymore would be dangerous.

Very dangerous.

"Shelbs. You're not gonna believe this. Your mama surprised me with two tickets to the Fourth of July race. We're going to Daytona. I've wanted to go to Daytona my whole life. The 500 costs way too much, but she scrimped and saved for a while now and I'm just as happy to be going in July. Can you believe it Shelbs?"

I'm not believing much of anything at this point. He's finally going to Daytona. Why now? Why this year?

I don't know why I'm so nervous. It's not like I'm going to be there or anything. It's not like Court will be there.

Putting as much enthusiasm in my voice as I can, I answer my dad. "That's great news, Dad. I know you'll have an awesome time."

"Your mama, she's got such a big heart. And you're just like her."

A big heart and a deceiving heart. That's what I have.

I am standing in the yard of Cal Treyhune, my dad's hero in life. And I can't say a word.

I can't say a word because there are way too many scenarios which could play out, and if even one of them did, I would be exposed for who I really am.

"I'm excited for sure, Shelbs."

A high-pitched squeal rings out in the air. I turn toward the house and see Bristol and Darling running out the door. "Dad, I need to run. The kids I'm watching are up, and I need to get to work."

"They make you work on a Sunday? Don't you have a day off?"

"It's kind of round the clock right now. But it's okay. Tell Mama I said hi and I love her. You too. Talk to you soon."

"Love you, too. And yes, we'll talk soon."

We hang up, and I walk over to where Darling is chasing Bristol. "What are you girls doing? You can't be screaming through the house. Your grandpa needs to rest."

"Bristol took the last bagel. And I want it. She won't share, either."

I stand, hands on hips, and watch as Bristol shoves a bite of the bagel into her mouth. The bite is way too big and her mouth is working hard trying to chew it.

Taking Darling by the hand I start walking. "Come on, we'll find you something to eat."

Instead of wringing her hand out of mine, she actually squeezes my hand a little as we walk. She halfway turns and I see her stick her tongue out at Bristol, who immediately starts following us.

"Here," she says catching up and shoving the rest of the bagel in Darling's face. "I'll share."

"No. Shelby is going to make me breakfast."

Good grief, did I say I would make something? I don't think so, but since it seems to have calmed Darling down, I don't argue.

"I want Shelby to make me breakfast, too."

Bristol is keeping strides with us. We all walk into the kitchen, which is now void of Crystal. Her empty coffee cup and wrinkled paper still sit on the table. As Darling slides into a chair, Bristol drops what is left of her bagel into the trash can.

"Seriously?" I look at her. "Why did you throw away perfectly good food? There are starving children—"

"All over the world. I know."

And the rich people say it as well. "Well, there are. You had no reason to throw that away."

"I wanna eat what you cook. Like Darling."

With those words, she scoots a chair close to Darling and sits.

Opening the refrigerator and cabinets, I find an abundance of food and start cooking.

"What is going on here?"

The girls are still sitting in their chairs at the table as Court walks in. I'm standing at the stove, void of makeup, wearing a now grease-splattered shirt as I made the mistake of trying to cook the bacon too fast.

So glad I'm only the nanny. "Just cooking a little breakfast. Want some?"

He peruses the counter and stove, lifting a paper towel that covers the toast I've been making. As if on cue, the toaster oven beeps indicating another two slices are done.

Raising his eyebrows, he nods toward the toaster oven. Without asking, he takes the slices out and starts buttering them with the butter I had sitting next to the plate.

I don't say anything, but do appreciate his help. Finishing up the bacon, I pour the eggs that are ready to scramble into a pan, the sizzle breaking the quiet of the room.

"Something smells good."

The voice of Cal Treyhune halts my hand in mid-motion as I stir the eggs. After a moment, I start again, making sure the eggs don't burn. If I do this right they will come out fluffy and soft.

"Turns out Shelby is one good cook, Dad. Do you want some breakfast?"

"You bet I do. Bacon, eggs, my kind of food. You're a good woman, Shelby. A good woman with a good name to match."

Cal sits at the end of the table, and I wonder how much of the food I'm cooking he's even allowed to eat.

I don't say anything. I can't.

Images of my father blast into my mind.

Here I am, on Father's Day, making breakfast for the man my father considers his hero.

An unsettling feeling rolls through my stomach. I have no concrete reason to feel this way, but this life I'm living, mingling with the Treyhunes for the summer, is going to change my life.

I just don't know exactly how.

MISTRUSTS

THE DAY SPENT at the Treyhune compound proved to be exhausting. As we arrive home, the girls are sleepy and weepy and already missing their cousins.

It was a bad time to mention their hair.

A really bad time.

"If I start at the bottom and work my way up, it won't hurt. I promise."

You'd think I'd just asked them to give up their iPods instead of asking them if I could brush their hair.

"We don't want you to brush our hair." Bristol speaks for Team Twin.

"Girls." I sit at the end of the bed they are sitting on and they move a few feet toward the headboard, like I'm dangerous. "It's got to happen sometime. Those tangles must be brushed out."

"We can get the tangles out, see?" Bristol starts poking her fingers in her hair. She grimaces as her fingers collide with a tangled mass, but pushes through. Darling copies Bristol and starts yanking her hair as well.

"Good job, girls. Keep at it."

Court's voice pierces the room and we all look toward the door where Court is standing. His gaze drifts from the girls to me, where he nods his head toward the kitchen.

I look at the girls. "I'll be back."

Brush in hand, I follow Court to the kitchen. "Have they always brushed their hair with their hands?"

"Look. I know it seems strange, but MaryLeigh always let them do what they wanted with their hair."

Pressing my lips together I try to figure out how to say what I want to say without being disrespectful to Court or MaryLeigh, may she rest in peace.

"I can see how that would be all right when they were little," I say, not seeing at all. "But they are becoming young women, now. Their hair is long and probably beautiful, but who can tell?"

"Young women? They're ten."

"Ten today, thirteen tomorrow. It will be here before you know it."

"Can't we let nature take its course here? By the time they are thirteen I'm sure I won't be able to drag them away from the mirror."

Before I can answer, Bristol and Darling come running down the hall, bursting into the kitchen with an air of exuberance.

"Look," Bristol says, running fingers through part of the bottom of her hair. "It's working. No more tangles."

Darling hasn't been as successful as Bristol, but is still smiling and pretending that she has.

I now realize this battle is bigger than the hair. This has to do with MaryLeigh and hanging on to ways and ideas that she implemented, even if they weren't practical or even right.

Setting the brush on the bar stool I walk to Bristol and smooth my hand over the bottom of her hair. "Very nice. You've done a great job."

She smiles and so does Darling.

Court? I wouldn't call his expression smiling or happy. I'd call it more like he's trying to figure out what I'm up to.

As if I have a clue.

"DO YOU HAVE A minute?"

I'm sitting on my bed checking my email but look up when Court's voice interrupts my browsing. There are still people sending me emails regarding my former CFO job, and it's all I can do not to delete them.

Instead I've been forwarding them on to Dale's email. I'm surprised at how little emotion I have looking at his name. It's like the man of my dreams hadn't even been in the picture of my life ever.

"Sure." I set my laptop on the bed and follow Court, trying to decide which one of the many topics he wants to discuss with me. The homeschooling, the hair, the deceased wife's strange life ways, or the deceased wife's secrets.

He walks into the living room, a place I haven't spent much time. He chooses one of the chairs to sit in, so I choose the other, leaving us facing each other. He looks in place with his expensive attire settled into an expensive chair, covered in a soft cream-colored fabric.

"The girls like you a lot."

I can't tell by the expression on his face if he thinks this is a good thing or not. But it should be a good thing, so I'm going with that mindset. "I'm glad."

"They're different around you. Like me. I'm different around you. Which leaves me wondering what it is about you that has captured our attention?"

My stomach flutters at his words. This topic wasn't on my agenda of topics.

He stands, shoves his hands in his pockets, and slowly paces, his gaze on the floor as if looking at me might provide an answer that he doesn't want to receive.

I must say if he's playing stump the nanny, he has won this round.

"If you're expecting an answer, I don't know what to say. I'm not magic and I don't cast spells."

I think his eyes are smiling even if he isn't. "I've told you before you're pretty. Too pretty to be a witch."

"Thank you."

Totally out of what I've determined to be his character, he perches on the wide arm of the couch. This is something I would yell at the girls for, but he paid for all this furniture, so he can sit if he wants.

But I bet Mrs. Stratton would have something to say about it.

"Barb told me about your situation in Atlanta. Why you wanted to get away for a while. It's no good when something isn't what you think it is. It's even worse when somebody isn't who you thought they were."

At this point I, the queen of being somebody I'm not, try not to break out in a visible sweat.

I guess he takes my silence as an invitation to move forward with what is on his mind. "A broken engagement is hard, but it's better to find out before the marriage takes place. Trust me, I know."

He's not asking me questions, so I don't feel like I can ask him any questions. It's obvious though that his marriage wasn't the perfect picture the media painted it.

And Jared played a part in all this.

What part I can only guess.

So the sad, lonely widower Barb portrayed to me when she told me about this job probably isn't as sad as she thinks he is.

Or maybe he is. But the sadness might come from other places in addition to his wife's death. "Break-ups are deaths on a smaller scale."

And yes, I did just voice those words. Words that sounded great when they ran through my head, but I'm not so sure how great they sound to a man who is still grieving the death of his wife.

Or grieving the death of who he thought she was.

"Much smaller, but yes."

I'll give him that. I shiver, hoping I haven't belittled his situation in any way. "The point is we've both lost something. We just lost it in different ways."

"Someone, not something."

Maybe he was more vested than I was. I shrug.

He stands, walking toward me. He holds his hand out, like I need help. I wasn't aware I needed helped out of the chair.

But it appears I do.

His touch is gentle. The problem comes in that instead of letting go of my hand, he strengthens his grip and pulls me close to him. Unable to resist, I look into his eyes. A whole section of the wall he hides behind has eroded, and I can see way more than I want to as I drown in his gaze.

His lips move so I know he's speaking, but it takes a few seconds for the words to sink into my brain.

And when they do, I almost wish I'd stayed oblivious.

"Maybe one day we'll find another something."

"Maybe."

Sometimes silence can be awkward, but right now it seems right. I let it linger before asking if I heard him right. "Something or someone?" My words are whispered in the silence of the big house, my gaze never leaving his.

His lips finally curve into that smile I've been waiting to be the recipient of, and I'm thankful for his support as the word swoon enters into my mind.

"I think we'll be able to determine that when it happens."

MY FEET POUND THE pavement harder than ever the next morning. Sleep broken by visions of a handsome man plagued me all night long, until I knew I'd be better off not even trying anymore.

I know that after last night everything has changed. Court's implication is clear, and while I don't think he's ready to have another relationship, he wants to let me know he is well on his way to that point.

Maybe he's enamored by Team Twin liking me. The vibe I'm getting is that they haven't liked anyone who has been their teacher or nanny since MaryLeigh died.

And honestly, if Court hadn't told me they liked me I wouldn't have known.

There are a lot of ghosts in every closet of the Treyhune home. Way too many bones rattling together at the same time. I'd be a fool to become involved in all of their lives.

Too late.

As each foot hits the pavement it screams the phrase until "too late" pounds through my head, one word right after another.

I stop running as if that will stop the words.

It doesn't.

They simply come as I breathe in and out.

Too. Late.

The skies are gray this Monday morning. Showers threaten while thunder rumbles in the distance. The breeze doesn't help cool me down. It only fuels the rapid pace of my thoughts in directions I can't believe they are going.

Court Treyhune.

In a million years I never would have thought he'd be accompanying me on a morning run. Plaguing my thoughts.

Making me think happiness could come again so soon.

But the scales on this are way off balance. Weighing heavier than the promise of happiness, are past hurts and mistrusts.

.

MEMORIES

BRISTOL, DARLING AND I plow through the day. The rain came again making it impossible to go outside. I decided to take on the task of cleaning their rooms. They were excited at first, but soon became bored.

"But I want to keep that. Don't throw it away," Bristol whines.

I hold up the electronic learning device. "I'm not throwing it away. This is the box to give away. And this is for two-year-olds. You are way past this."

"But these are my toys." She grabs it out of my hands and hugs it to her chest.

"Girls. You have so many toys here that you've out grown. Can't you share them with others? Some parents can't afford to buy toys like these for their children."

I'm amazed at what these two have stored up. It's like they've never gotten rid of anything.

Whereas Court can't get rid of his memories, these girls can't get rid of their stuff.

They're all holding onto the past in different ways.

It's like their hair. I can see progress being made in the tangles. But I still want to grab a brush and be done with it.

"Some kids don't have toys?" Darling asks.

I nod. "That's right. Some kids don't."

"What do they play with?" Bristol asks.

Remembering back to my childhood, I have visions of jumping rope and using tree limbs pretending they were weapons. I also remember one year wanting a popular doll for Christmas.

It was all I wanted.

"Do you want to hear a story?" I ask.

They shrug. "Sure."

"When I was a little girl, about your age, there was a doll all the girls wanted. Her name was Pretty Patty."

Bristol smiles. "Was she pretty?"

"Of course she was. All I wanted for Christmas was a Pretty Patty doll. When Christmas morning came there was only one box for me under the tree. I still remember how excited I was when I opened the box and saw Pretty Patty."

"So Santa brought you what you wanted."

"He did. But later in the day I noticed the box was a little banged up, and the flaps looked well worn. Later that night, I was in bed, hugging Pretty Patty close to me. While I was hugging her I noticed a smudged pen mark on the side of her left cheek."

"Someone wrote on her? Why?"

"It was probably an accident. But that doll hadn't been out of my arms all day long, so I knew I hadn't done it. I rubbed the mark as hard as I could, but the blue smudge wouldn't go away." I decline telling them that even my tears falling on Pretty Patty's face didn't help take the mark away.

"So what did you do?" Darling asks.

"I just loved her even though she had the mark on her face."

Team Twin look at me with wide eyes.

"I never would have had Pretty Patty if some nice girl like you hadn't given her away. So what do you say? Can we pick out some toys that you don't play with anymore and give them to some other little girls?"

Their eyes take on an excited look. They jump up and walk over to the pile of toys. "Sure."

"I'll help." As I stand I see a shadow out of the corner of my eye. Looking toward the door my face turns red and my head starts to spin as I see Court leaning in the doorway, arms crossed, with a half-smile on his face.

Mrs. Stratton indicated he never came home early, and it's barely mid-afternoon. I would never have told my story if I thought there was a remote possibility that he would be around.

Thankfully, Bristol and Darling are busy picking out toys. It's bad enough the drama being played out in my head and heart is being witnessed by Court. Certainly he can see my turmoil at revealing sacred secrets of my past.

A past I never wanted him to know anything about.

But it appears my charade is up. He motions for me to come to him.

As I reach him, he steps outside the door and I follow. He's smiling which surprisingly puts me at ease. Probably because it took me so long to be on the receiving end of one of those.

When I reach him, he puts his hand on my shoulder, once again reeling me in to a comfortable place. "That was great. You didn't tell me you were a master storyteller."

All thoughts of asking him why he came home early leave my mind. A master storyteller? Because I related a piece of my childhood to the girls? "I don't think I'm a master storyteller by any means."

"Are you kidding me? The way you had them wrapped up in that tale? You almost had me believing it for a minute. It sounded so real. And it brought them around. They can't shove toys in that box fast enough."

I'm not sure whether I should feel the relief I'm feeling.

He doesn't believe I'm the poor kid who wouldn't have Christmas if it wasn't for second-hand stores.

He thinks my memories are tales?

For the first time, my heart tells me that Court would understand. That Court is different from Paul in high school and from Dale. I want to believe he is.

I really do.

But I can't embrace it yet. I continue to let Court think my story is just that.

A made-up story. "I'm glad I was convincing." There. That doesn't confirm or deny anything. He came to his own conclusions without any prompting from me.

But somehow my conscious isn't cleared by my statement at all.

In fact, it's more conflicted now than ever.

"SO, IF I SEND Mrs. Stratton home will you cook us some fried chicken, mashed potatoes and gravy?"

Court catches me as I step out of my room just a few minutes after our previous conversation. The conversation that caused me to splash cold water on my face to wake up to the reality of what is happening.

I did this while the girls showed Court what they were doing and why. Their excitement at sharing their toys was almost as grand as seeing their dad home midday.

"Fried chicken is not very healthy eating. I think we should let Mrs. Stratton do her stuff."

"Only if you give me an IOU." There's a serious look in his expression.

"Maybe." I'm not committing to anything.

Rubbing his neck, he stares at the hallway wall for a moment like he's bothered. Moments later, he looks at me. "Can we talk for a minute? In my office?"

My breath hitches slightly. Nothing he would notice. But I'm catching on to his voice tones, and this one indicates turmoil.

What kind of turmoil I'm about to find out.

He follows me, and when he steps into the office he shuts the door behind him.

In my book, that inches up the turmoil factor.

Now my mouth is starting to feel dry. Why does everything having to do with Court make me aware of every internal struggle I have? It's like being around him forces me to see more of who I am.

Who I really am.

And that's not at all who I want to be.

Maybe it's because Court is a what-you-see-is-what-you-get type of guy. There's not any pretense when it comes to him.

Only amazing honesty and integrity.

Traits to be admired.

"You can sit if you want." He perches on the edge of the desk while motioning me to the love seat.

My nerves are too crazy to sit, so I don't. He raises his eyebrows, but doesn't comment on my refusal of his offer.

"Before we left North Carolina yesterday, my dad asked me to do him a favor."

My nerve endings quit tingling a little as I realize this talk is going to be about Court and his dad and not about Court and me.

My nerve endings are also a tad bit disappointed.

But they won't tell anyone.

"What kind of favor?"

"The kind of favor I wish he wouldn't have asked."

Those words tell a tale, don't they? "I hate those kind of favors. Especially when asked by someone you love. Kind of makes it hard to say no, doesn't it?"

"Impossible, really."

"So what does your dad have you doing that you don't really want to do?"

He pushes off the desk and stands, lowering his gaze momentarily. When he does look up, his gaze captivates me more than I want it to.

"He wants me to go to the track for the Fourth of July race at Daytona."

Oh, that race. That race that my dad has graciously been given tickets to by Mama. "Why?"

"Because he can't go. Storm is usually with him, but that's his anniversary and he and the wife are taking a vacation. So my dad wants me to fill in for the weekend."

I shake my head. "How did Storm get away with getting married in the middle of the season? I thought they all got married and had babies in the winter, when they weren't racing."

Once again his eyebrows raise which instantly clue me in to my error. And once again, I've just revealed that I know something about this sport. I need to think fast. "I'm just assuming of course." Maybe that will cover up my faux pas.

"Of course." His tone implies anything but. "Storm and Renney were only thinking in the moment. They weren't thinking about forty-year anniversaries back then."

"Guess not."

"So, anyway, Dad wants me to hit the track that week."

I continue to relax as the conversation proceeds. Court will be at the track. The girls and I will be here. My dad will still be none the wiser. "So, I guess you're going."

He leans against the desk, and I love how he looks in his black slacks and gray button up shirt. Once again, he's barely rolled up his sleeves. He's also loosened his tie just a little. Everything about him screams expensive.

And hot.

"We're going."

"We're?"

He points at me then back at himself. "Yes. We're. And Bristol and Darling. We'll make it fun."

Fun? His idea of fun and my idea of fun are different. My dad. My dad.

Those are the only words running through my mind.

They start to slow realizing my dad and I will not be traveling in the same circles at the race track. My life goal achieved.

But I never thought I'd be at any race track at the any time.

My nightmare achieved.

"How will it be fun for us if you are working?"

"Have you ever been to a race?"

"Are you kidding me?" I didn't mean for it to come across sounding negative, but his expression indicates it was.

"Well, then, you are in for an experience. The girls will be excited, but we're not telling them until it's closer to the time. We won't be able to live with them if we tell them now."

We're. We. The words roll out of his mouth like they are nothing. Like we're a couple making a decision together.

"It should be interesting." My gaze drifts to the homeschool information still sitting on Court's desk. The file folders filled with mostly useless information. That whole thing is interesting as well.

The checks and financial statements are gone. Must be at the office.

"We'll stay in the motor home. We won't have a cook though. You up for that? I'm still thinking of your fried chicken."

"I don't think a motor home is the best place to be frying chicken."

"You haven't seen this motor home. You'll think you are in a house."

I place my hands on either side of my head. Like pushing on it will erase this conversation we've just had. I can't believe the turn this has taken.

I'm actually going to be at a NASCAR race with the family that made the sport famous.

And I can't tell a soul.

MESSAGE

MRS. STRATTON shakes her head at the sound of the garage door opening.

At mid-afternoon once again.

"Two days in a row that man has come home early." She narrows her eyes at me, but not in a bad way.

More like a suspicious way.

The girls are watching a movie in their room and I am grabbing a snack since I somehow missed eating lunch.

I look away from Mrs. Stratton, finding my gaze drifting toward the hallway that Court will be walking up momentarily. Unbelievably, I find myself counting the seconds until he appears.

Whoa. Where did that come from and why?

I try to shift my gaze, but that doesn't last. As I focus back on the hallway, he appears, once again dressed impeccably.

"Ladies?"

"Hello, Mr. Treyhune. To what do we owe the unexpected pleasure of your early arrival for the second day in a row?" Mrs. Stratton tone drips sarcasm.

He drops some mail on the counter. "Since the rain has cleared out, I thought I'd take my girls to the boardwalk, grab an early dinner, and hang out."

While I feel a pang of disappointment in not being included, I realize I'll actually have some time to myself. Time that I'm not supposed to be sleeping. It will be nice. Maybe I can make a couple of phone calls. Catch up on my social media that I've been totally ignoring since seeing a picture of Dale and his new girl on a mutual friend's page.

Insensitive friend.

Dale's friend whom I've since unfriended.

"So," he starts, looking at me, "if you can get the girls ready, we'll leave in about thirty minutes. I need to answer a couple of emails that came over while I was driving and then change my clothes."

"Sure. They're watching a movie, but they'll be much more excited to go with you."

His hand inches toward mine on the counter, but stops short of touching me. "What about you? Are you excited?"

Smiling, I wonder why he made the effort to move close to me, but didn't touch me. "I'm excited about having a couple of hours to myself, I guess."

"Yourself? You're going to ditch us once we get there?"

"Oh." My hand retracts to my lap, removing all possibility of touching him. "I thought you were just taking Team Twin."

"Team Twin?"

He laughs as I remember that I haven't clued him in on my nickname for the girls. "Yeah. Team Twin. Do you like it?"

"I do. It sounds like you."

Mrs. Stratton clears her throat. Both Court and I look at her. We can't see her face as she is not facing us, but it looks like her shoulders are tensed up.

Did Court's words cause that?

Court walks over to Mrs. Stratton. He places his hands on the counter next to where she is standing. "I hope you're not in the middle of making us some big, fancy dinner."

Her knife makes a loud noise as it scrapes the cutting board. "No. I'm cutting vegetables. They'll keep until tomorrow night. You go and have your date night with your *girls*."

The way she says the word girls makes my body tingle. Like I'm Court's girl. I like the way my body tingles, though.

The doorbell rings, squelching all thoughts of tingling. Mrs. Stratton sets the knife on the cutting board before wiping her hands on a towel she has hanging from her apron.

"I'll get it," Court says.

Mrs. Stratton resumes cutting whatever green vegetable she was cutting while Court heads to the door. As he passes by me, his cool, crisp scent breezes by making me think of the word tingle all over again.

The sound of Jared's voice squelches it.

When Court and Jared walk into the kitchen I try to smile.

Jared's presence puts a damper on the mood that Court created by talking about a fun evening out. Maybe Jared won't stay long.

"How's my Stones date?" He walks to me and gives me a hug, drenching me with his overpowering scent. I hug him back, reluctantly, remembering Court's words about being jealous.

I find myself very aware of Court's tension that I'm sure Jared doesn't know exists. I would like to think it's all about me, but I think there's more to it.

"You have the day off?" Court asks.

"Not the day. Got to work at the crack of dawn. But I'm off the rest of the day. Good behavior."

"I'm sure." Court's light tone sounds forced.

"So, I thought I'd come by and see what was shaking around here. I'm surprised to find you here, actually," Jared says to Court.

"I live here."

"Noted. You also normally work fifteen hour days."

"Noted," Court replies. "So you thought I wouldn't be here."

"Busted."

"Well, you may have the afternoon off, but Shelby doesn't. She's working for a few more hours."

Jared laughs. "Come on. All work isn't good for anybody."

"Shelby likes her work." Court's tone challenges Jared to disagree.

Not wanting to be drawn into this conversation, I take this opportunity to scoot down the hall where the girls are watching the movie. When I tell them we are going out, they jump up, turn the movie off and start putting on their shoes.

"Go brush your hair—teeth if you didn't this morning." Their hair is coming along, but I'm still in awe of the situation. And, I don't tell them their dad is home yet. I would lose any sort of authority I have right now.

I'm still in my room stalling when the girls burst in.

"We're ready. Where are we going?"

"It's a surprise, Bristol." As I speak her name I realize I didn't look down at the band to see who was speaking.

A small sense of accomplishment washes over me. I look at the girls realizing there are small differences that I now notice. Bristol tends to keep her hair tucked behind her ears, while Darling's is always hanging close to her face. Bristol's eyes have more of a defiant, narrowed look than wide-eyed Darling's.

"Look who's home."

Court's voice breaks into my Team Twin perusal. The girls run to Court as I finish putting my hair in a ponytail.

"Uncle Jared is here, too."

As I turn toward the door, the girls leave Court and latch on to Jared who is standing in the hall. Court's gaze catches mine. I know it's only seconds that pass, but his gaze sends a message that my heart understands, changing it forever.

It's as if a million words were spoken and many years passed by.

When I meet Court as he stands in my doorway, he takes my hand in his. As our fingers intertwine, and our palms meet, life makes sense for the first time.

He squeezes my hand before letting it go, and I know that squeeze is the beginning of something beautiful.

Before I can contemplate the tragedy of how the something beautiful will end, Team Twin rushes us. I know they didn't see Court hold my hand, but as I look over at Jared, I can't be sure if his gaze is hardened, or if I'm imagining it.

"Let's go," Court says, as he points down the hall. "There are entirely too many people in this hallway."

Jared leads the way to the garage, Team Twin behind him. Court motions for me to go in front of him.

He places his hands on my shoulders as we walk down the hall, dropping them when Jared reaches the door to the garage.

I guess this something beautiful is going to be a secret something beautiful.

I'm just not sure who we are keeping it a secret from.

Jared or Team Twin.

Or both.

THE BOARDWALK ISN'T crowded on this late Tuesday afternoon.

No, the only place there is too many people is in our group.

One too many.

Jared.

Jared who has tried a couple of times to pull me away from Court and the girls.

I notice Court noticing.

Whoa, this has become complicated.

Keeping the girls in line is simple compared to the tug of war between Court and Jared.

And I'm the rope.

"So, the Stones concert is Friday night. I'll pick you up at six. That way we can have dinner before the show." Jared's voice is loud, like he wants to make sure we all hear him. Even Court.

My stomach drops and I speak before thinking. "I don't get off work until at least seven. After the girls eat. Then it all depends on what time Court gets home."

Jared playfully punches Court in the forearm. "Court's coming home early that night, aren't you buddy."

"I'll try. That's the best I can do."

"It'll happen." Jared speaks his words confidently.

To say our group is garnishing looks as people pass by would be an understatement. These two guys are gorgeous and I wonder how many people know who Court is.

No one has asked for any autographs yet, but I'm not counting it out.

I'm trying to focus on Bristol and Darling. With my mind spinning way too many amazing thoughts of Court, then trying to keep Jared at bay, my task is difficult, but doable.

Right now Bristol is holding my left hand while Darling is holding my right hand.

The girls flourish in the presence of their father. They are ten times more well behaved. Bristol's eyes become less narrowed, while Darling's are not so wide-eyed.

It's like they are little girls with a simple mission of being little girls when Court is around.

Court and Jared are walking behind us. Occasionally the breeze will blow the scents of their cologne my way, Jared's overpowering Court's. But

I'm more aware of Court's.

"It's hot." Bristol tugs on my arm. "Can we get something to drink?"

I kind of turn my head to look at Court. Any excuse will do. "The girls are thirsty."

"Looks like some lemonade to our left just up ahead."

"Yeah!"

The girls release my grasp and take off toward the picture of the oversized lemon.

"So Jared," Court starts. "Any luck in finding more information on the loss of profits?"

"I haven't found much, but it looks like June is on track with the March statement."

"We're selling more cars. Of course June will be up. It should run away from March."

"Exactly. It's on track for doing that. Running away with it. Profit will be up. Way up."

I struggle to keep my mouth closed. While my eyes are watching Team Twin, not letting them out of my sight, my ears are hearing Jared's attempt at pacifying Court regarding his business.

I hope Court hears what I'm hearing and he's not letting Jared's vague explanations ring true.

But Jared is his best friend. Is Court's judgment clouded by that fact? Court obviously has issues with the fact that Jared never let on that he knew MaryLeigh from their childhood, but this talk is about the business.

Court's business.

Jared touches my forearm with his index finger. "Looks like you are getting burnt. Did you put any sunscreen on?"

I watch as my reddened skin turns white where the pressure of his finger was. The white fades and I have to admit that I didn't put on any sunscreen.

Nor did I put any on Bristol and Darling.

Bad nanny.

"I guess I forgot." I don't add anything about forgetting Team Twin.

Jared points to a souvenir shop. "I'll run in there and buy some."

"That's not necessary," I say, but Jared is already on his way.

"Lemonade?" Court asks, as his gaze follows Jared.

"Sure."

Bristol and Darling are standing next to me while Court purchases our cool drinks.

"Not thirsty?" I ask as he passes small drinks to the girls and a larger one to me.

"I thought we might share." He holds up two paper-wrapped straws.

"Okay."

The small drinks already have straws in them. He unwraps one straw and jams it through the hole. As he unwraps the other straw it drops out of his hand. He reaches down, picks it up then tosses it into the trash can. "Whoops. Guess we have to share."

"Guess so," I say, matching his smile.

His eyes dance with mine and for a moment I think we are the only two people on this earth.

"Jared to the rescue with sunscreen."

Jared's voice reminds me there are other people on the planet. I hold out my free hand offering to take the sunscreen. "Thanks."

"No." Jared holds tightly onto the bottle. "Let me."

"I don't think so, my friend." Court holds out his hand, his intention clear. "She's my nanny."

MISERABLE

THE WORD I WOULD use to describe Court's gaze is smoldering.

I'm not sure what word Jared would use.

Team Twin?

They're happy in their lemonade and oblivious to the adult drama being played out a foot away from them.

Court takes the bottle from Jared. "And she's capable of putting on her own sunscreen." He switches the bottle for the drink.

"Then I need to put some on the girls." Drama resolved, but my arms were looking forward to Court's touch in those few seconds I thought he was going to offer to lathe the lotion on me.

"I see how it is." Jared laughs like we are all playing a joke. The thing is, we all know it's not a joke, but a power play.

As much as I'll admit to myself I'm attracted to Court, and I feel like he's attracted to me, that's not something the world needs to know. Jared being part of the world.

So, what is looking like a power play isn't really one. But the stress of it is still there.

"The lemonade is good, Daddy."

Darling nods as Bristol speaks.

After rubbing lotion on my arms, then the girls, I try to hand it back to Jared.

"No. Keep it. My treat."

"Thanks." I drop the lotion into my purse firmly aware of Jared's frustration.

And considering he invited himself along, I don't care that he's frustrated.

Another part of me is thankful that he came by. I'm not sure what passed between me and Court would have passed if it wasn't for Jared's impromptu visit.

PEEKING INTO BRISTOL'S room, I see the girls sound asleep, their hair spread across the bed. If I thought I could get away with it, I'd take my brush in there and handle that situation.

But I know there's no way that would go unnoticed.

Besides, the anticipation of being alone with Court after today's events has my anticipation level at heights I've never known.

Even with Dale.

If I told Mama all this she would say it was the Lord working. She would say He made sure Dale and I didn't get married because Dale wasn't the one I was supposed to be with for the rest of my life.

Look at my mind. Going here and there. Places just weeks ago I never thought it would go again.

And I may be keyed up for nothing. I have no idea where Court is. He might have even gone to bed.

But I doubt it.

I hope not.

I walk into the kitchen, the silence indicating there is no one around.

Before a sense of total disappointment can engulf me, I notice the door to the terrace not quite shut.

Knowing Mrs. Stratton would never leave one door unlocked, I know Court is outside.

Or was.

I'm betting he wouldn't leave the door like that if he had come back inside.

With a bold sense of confidence, I walk toward the door, unsure of what lies on the other side.

This door doesn't creak like I hope it will, so now it's up to me to announce my own presence.

I see Court sitting by the pool. He's sitting on a bench seat with plenty of room for two, which excites me on one hand, and scares me on the other.

He still doesn't notice me.

"Would you like to join me?"

Oh.

Maybe he does.

Pulling the door tight, I walk the few steps that separate me from Court. Soft lights glow as the moon is backing off its fullness from the night in the mountains.

Lowering myself next to Court, I notice my hands shake a little as I brace them on the bench.

I also notice Court watching me.

"I had fun today."

I like the sound of his voice. "Me, too."

"Better than sitting behind my desk."

"Much better," I add, refusing to think about all the days I've spent behind a desk and away from the sunshine.

His fingers touch my hair. "I like the smell of your shampoo."

He should. I pay over twenty dollars for one bottle. "Thanks."

"Can't place the scent, though. Some kind of fruit?"

I shrug, not looking at him. "I'm not sure."

"I want to kiss you. May I?"

Slivers of chills cover me at his soft words. I've never had anyone ask to kiss me before. It's kind of nice. "Yes," I respond probably much too quickly, but not caring as everything inside of me sears with anticipation of his lips on mine.

Will I stop breathing?

Melt?

Or simply come alive as I blossom into his kiss.

I feel his finger under my chin, turning my face toward him.

It's a good thing he's helping.

He leans toward me.

I close my eyes as I move to meet him.

His lips.

They touch mine and I tremble, wanting to wrap my arms around him and pull him close.

His hand cups the side of my face as he kisses me into a mind-numbing state where no thoughts exist because they are insignificant compared to the feel of who he is.

I place my hand on the back of his neck, my fingers reveling in the softness of his hair. It's like silk to my fingertips.

Our lips part.

My forehead rests against his, like this is what we do after we kiss. I have no words.

I have an ache.

An ache for his lips to be on mine.

I turn my head slightly and make that move. His breath hitches and I feel his heart beat as I move my hand to his chest, no shirt able to conceal the racing beneath.

In a swift movement, he scoops me onto his lap and I sit, legs dangling over his.

I fit perfectly.

We continue to kiss. Years of pent-up passion have been unleashed, waiting for this moment and this moment alone.

Nothing else exists right now except for our kisses.

Our discovery of each other.

His hands caress my hair, while his lips kiss their way over my chin, to my ear lobe then down my neck. Only to start again when I capture his lips in mine.

It's a cycle I don't want to end.

But as his lips nuzzle my neck, my brain pushes through the fog he has created.

And I rest.

I lean against his body, my head on his shoulder, as we both breathe in the night air.

His fingers gently trace mindless patterns on my arm which is slightly pink from our outing today.

My brain is telling me I should feel awkward or embarrassed, but I don't. I feel like I belong right here, in his lap, waiting for him to kiss me again.

And again.

"Can we sleep here?" His voice is husky, raw, like his kisses.

"I'm fine with it." I wrap my arm tighter around him, solidifying my words.

My words which came out raspy and breathless like I'm feeling inside.

"Just like this." He unwraps my arm from around him, brings my palm to his lips, and kisses it.

Softly.

He kisses it again and I can't fathom how I could feel any more than I'm feeling now if we were to continue this relationship. My whole body is about to burst from simply kissing him.

I give up my relaxed state to capture his lips. He responds with a need as strong as mine.

Like we're drinking water after a long thirst.

"Sleep is overrated," he whispers between kisses.

"Very overrated," I whisper back.

I want him to kiss me from my head to my toes, even though I don't think I'd live through it.

It would be worth dying for.

As he continues to melt me with his lips, my mind freight trains its way to months from now.

Days from now.

Hours from now.

Minutes.

He kisses me with abandonment. Like he's letting loose.

Like he's trying to rid himself of the same demons I'm trying to rid myself of.

I reluctantly end our kiss and instead, with only inches separating us, stare into his eyes.

"You okay?" he asks.

"Yes," I lie.

"I want to ask you to stay with me tonight."

My mind tumbles. "Court—"

His finger touches my lips, cutting off my words.

"But I want more than that. I want to know more about you. I want to know your favorite color, your favorite food. I already know your favorite wine."

And with those words, all the warmth he created that flows through my body turns to ice.

He knows nothing about me.

And what he thinks he knows, he doesn't.

"Tell me you want to know more about me. Tell me you're

interested."

The ice continues to flow as I want to scream I already know so much about you.

"Shelby, tell me."

"I…"

He cups my face, and crushes my lips with another amazing kiss which he ends quickly. "You don't kiss like we kiss when you don't feel."

I wiggle off his lap, the absence of him stronger than I had imagined. Once again, my hands tremble, but this time for a whole different reason. "The problem with kissing away the demons from the past is that we're creating new demons for the future."

Shivering, I rub my arms as I make my way to the door, each step harder than the last.

Each step making me more miserable.

Each step necessary.

MIND-BLOWING

I AWAKE EARLY the next morning, but I lie in bed until I hear Mrs. Stratton arrive and Court leave.

When the sound of his car is gone, I shower, wondering how I'm ever going to face him again.

I swear my lips are still swollen from his kisses.

Thinking of kisses inspires sensations I hadn't felt until last night.

It's funny the real feelings need can create.

He has a need.

I have a need.

Maybe we kissed our needs away in the dark of the night, and we can move forward now.

For a few hours yesterday I thought that life could be different. Easy. With Court.

But passion has a funny way of revealing truth.

And the truth is we both are plagued by our pasts.

And we can't have a future together.

Once in the kitchen I pour myself a much needed cup of coffee and gulp down a swig of the hot liquid.

"Slow down, honey. That'll burn your throat," Mrs. Stratton says.

I hold up my hand indicating I know what she says is true and slide onto a barstool.

Even the pain of the hot liquid on my tongue and then my throat can't erase the sensation of Court's amazing kisses.

"No running today?" she asks.

"No. Not today." My body had a workout last night, but I'm not telling Mrs. Stratton that.

"Mr. Treyhune looked like the devil himself this morning, all broody and scowling."

I raise my eyebrows.

"And you," she points to me, "look like the she-devil."

Resisting the urge to spew the coffee I just sipped, I shrug my shoulders.

"Never seen Mr. Treyhune in a state like this."

I know she wants me to ask "like what?" but I refuse. I'm not falling into her trap.

Instead I take another sip of coffee.

Mrs. Stratton walks to the refrigerator, opens it and pulls out the creamer I've been using. After she pours some into my coffee, keeping her eyes on mine, she sets the creamer by the coffee pot like I do each morning.

"Seems you're somewhat forgetful this morning."

"Seems so."

Forgetful, confused and falling in love.

This time I do spew my coffee.

"I'm sorry." I slide off the bar stool in search of a towel.

"Sit," she says, motioning to me. "Sit. I'll take care of it."

I take my place at the bar wishing Mrs. Stratton really could take care of it.

NEEDING A TOTAL distraction from not only Court, but the house, I drag the girls next door. I ring the doorbell as Bristol and Darling are both still protesting.

"We don't even know this girl or anyone who lives here. Talk about awkward." Bristol stomps her foot and crosses her arms.

Darling copies her, but with much less enthusiasm.

"I'm sure she's a very nice girl."

"Oh, this is embarrassing," Bristol says as the front door opens.

"Can I help you?" a woman dressed in a uniform much like Mrs. Stratton's asks.

"Yes," I say, realizing how right Bristol is. This is awkward. But it's better than being in the Treyhune mansion today. "Is Jenny or Stephen here?"

"They are. May I tell them who's calling?"

"We're not calling. We're standing here," Bristol says.

I give Bristol a look, but she doesn't recognize it as a look. "Calling can mean different things. Not just the phone. I apologize," I say to the woman. "We're the neighbors. Actually, they're the neighbors." I point to Bristol and Darling. "I'm the nanny."

The nanny that kissed their very handsome yet off limits father until she was senseless last night. That nanny.

My face reddens as my lips tingle at the memory of last night's intimacy.

"Come in. I'll tell them you're here."

We follow the woman to the living room and sit on the couch as she disappears. Moments later, Stephen and Jenny come into the room, followed by a girl that looks to be the same age as Team Twin.

Her hair is dark like Team Twin, but it's cut above her shoulders in a cute bob. No tangles.

Easy to maintain, I bet.

"Hi, Shelby. Good to see you again." Stephen nods toward the girls. "I see you've brought the twins over."

"I have. As promised."

"We're glad you did," Jenny says, putting her arm around the girl that came in with them. "This is Phoebe."

"Hi, Phoebe. I've brought Bristol and Darling over. Us grown-ups thought you guys might like to play together, or hang out, whatever it's called now."

"I'd like that, but we're getting ready for vacation Bible school."

"What's that?" Bristol asks.

Boy, these kids have been sheltered. "It's when a lot of kids get together and learn stories from the Bible. It's usually lasts about a week."

Jenny smiles. "Ours is less than a week. We're actually starting tomorrow and going through Saturday morning. The kids are putting on a show Sunday morning. Hey, Bristol and Darling should come." Jenny looks at me like it's the most natural thing in the world for Team Twin to jump in.

"I'll have to talk it over with their dad." Oh, which means I'll have to face him.

And not kiss him.

Redirection of thoughts needed immediately.

"Do you girls want to come and see what we have ready so far? We could always use an extra set of helping hands." Jenny rests her hand on Phoebe's shoulder.

"Helping?" Bristol looks at me. "Like we helped those kids who didn't have any toys?"

"Yes. That's helping. Would you girls like to help Phoebe?"

Bristol shrugs. "I guess."

Phoebe holds out her hand. "Come on."

Bristol looks perplexed. "I'm over here."

"Phoebe's blind," Jenny says.

"Blind? You mean you can't see with your eyes?" Darling asks.

"No, I can't."

"Wow." Bristol's eyes are now Darling-wide. "I've never met a blind person before. This is cool."

"I'm just like you, but I can't see. I'm sure there are things you can't do, aren't there?"

"I guess," Bristol says.

"Let's go, then." Stephen looks at me. "Come on back. We'll show you around."

We all traipse down the hall and enter a room that used to be a garage. But now it's carpeted, and painted. There's even a stage built at one end.

Small tables are set up with chairs around them. Booklets are on the table along with crayons and papers.

"Cool," Bristol says, sliding into one of the chairs.

"Oh, no." I tap Bristol on the top of her head. "That's for tomorrow, I'm sure. Get up."

Jenny waves her hand in the air. "She can color. We have plenty of paper."

Now Bristol gives me a look and starts coloring.

"Guess you'll miss out on helping then," I say to Bristol.

"There's plenty to do," Jenny says. "We were just about to organize the snacks, weren't we Phoebe?"

"We were. Do you guys want to help?" Phoebe asks.

"I do," Darling says.

Bristol continues to sit and color while Darling follows Phoebe and Jenny.

"If you need a break, you can leave them. Come back in about an hour or so?"

He has no idea this is my break. Being around Team Twin and now Stephen, Jenny and Phoebe keep my thoughts away from Court and all that transpired last night.

And that crazy thought about love this morning.

Although watching Stephen watch Jenny is love happening in the present. The way they look at each other practically heats the air around them. I wonder what it's like to be secure in a love like that.

I never felt that way with Dale.

Thinking about my mom and dad, I realize they love like this. Hard and true and without doubt. Not that there aren't any hard times, but knowing your heart is secure in someone else's must be amazing.

Must make pushing through the tough times worth it. And as a couple you come out stronger through the fire than when you started into it.

That's the kind of love I want.

And I'm not going to find that with Court.

"Shelby, will you stay?"

I look at Bristol, her hair behind her ears, eyes pleading with me. "Yes. I'll stay."

She smiles and continues to color.

"Well, if you're staying we can use your help."

"I'll do whatever." Anything to keep my mind away from Court Treyhune.

I PUT THE GIRLS to bed even though they haven't seen their father. It's a little after nine, and they are exhausted. We stayed at Jenny and Stephen's for almost three hours and left with a promise to be back in the morning at eight for vacation Bible school providing Court doesn't have any objections.

I should call him.

Although I hate calling when it isn't an emergency.

Somehow talking to him on the phone seems just as awkward as it will be to see him in person.

Maybe even more so, because he might read things into the phone call that aren't there.

Or are there, but I don't want him to know.

No, it's best to face him. In fact, it might be a great icebreaker into segueing things back to where they were before he kissed life into me.

I settle in his office with the homeschooling files. I notice the financial statements and check copies he had printed out are on the other desk, the one with the computer on it.

I look at the financial statements. He's printed six months worth, and things were steady until April. May looks even worse.

Quickly locating the payroll accounts, I find those expenses went up a little each month. So, while overall profits have gone down, payroll expenses have not.

And neither have the other expenses.

Advertising has almost doubled.

Did Court notice that?

I'm sure he did. That's the account a couple of those checks were posted to.

Placing the financials back where I found them, I realize I need to quit being concerned about his business. It's none of my business. He's been doing this without me for many years.

Still, as I look through the homeschool items, my mind keeps drifting back to numbers that don't make sense.

"Hi."

As much as I've prepared all day to hear his voice, I find I'm not prepared at all for the sound of it.

"Hi." Even though I'm sitting at his desk, I don't feel protected by it. His presence shatters any barrier I might have imagined between us.

His gaze captures mine and doesn't let go. "I waited for you this morning."

He did? "I overslept."

"On purpose?"

"Maybe."

"You kind of crushed me last night the way you left. Good thing I don't have an ego."

What made me think I could avoid this topic? What made me think we could pretend last night didn't happen and pick up with Team Twin's schedule and issues? "I thought I explained myself."

He chuckles. "Your explanation required an explanation. Demons? Really?"

"You know what I'm talking about."

He sits on the loveseat. "I'm not sure that I do. When I was kissing you, all I could picture in my mind was your face. Your beautiful face. What were you picturing?"

"You, of course." This isn't going my way at all. He's missing the point.

"Will you come over here and sit by me?"

"Will you kiss me?"

"Probably."

"At least you're honest." I push back from the desk wishing my heart would listen to my brain as I make my way to where Court sits. His pull is strong and it seems useless to sit next to him, so I move his arm and sit in his lap hoping he'll kiss me immediately.

The anticipation will kill me otherwise.

And he does.

The urgency of last night has been replaced by knowing more about him. Knowing that his lips will fit mine perfectly and kiss me senseless has me drowning in his warmth.

His arms hold me captive as if I would try to leave.

I should. My brain tells me this. My brain also told me to avoid him this morning which made me angsty all day. Bad brain.

After too many kisses for my own good, we stop.

I'm breathless once again.

"You were on my mind all day."

His words slowly sink in. "You, too. On mine."

Broken sentences, broken brain.

We rest.

Together.

We don't kiss.

We don't speak.

I don't trust myself to say anything. I still believe what I said last night, I really do. But a few kisses will surely not a relationship make, right?

I'm leaving in a couple of months. And I'm not going to do anything but kiss Court, that's a given.

Why deny myself the pleasure this man brings me because of things that haven't even crossed his mind? "I have a question for you."

I feel him stiffen as I speak. "Yes?"

"Can Team Twin go to vacation Bible school tomorrow next door at Stephen and Jenny's house?"

"What?" he asks. "Where did this come from?"

I sit up straighter in his lap so I can see his gorgeous face. "I took the girls over there this afternoon, and they were setting up for vacation Bible school which starts tomorrow and goes through Sunday. Well, Saturday, but the kids are doing a program Sunday morning. Bristol and Darling helped set up and they want to go. Is it okay?"

He traces a line down my nose. "So, I pay you to watch my girls and you take them next door for a few days."

"That's how it works."

"I say yes."

"Great."

"On one condition."

Now it's my turn to trace a line down his nose. "And what would that be?"

"That you hang out with me while they are there."

Now I stiffen. He can't be serious. "But you're at work."

"I'll work from home."

"What will I do while you work?"

"This." He pulls me toward him and kisses me. Not once, not twice, but three long, sexy, amazing kisses.

"That's what goes on at your work?"

He tucks my hair behind my ears. "I'll take a break or two."

"Oh. I'm your break."

"Shelby, you're intelligent. Beautiful. Great with the kids. Why can't you admit there might be something between us?"

Instead of answering, I kiss him. Slowly, passionately, Court's kisses send me to another level, spiraling mindlessly into him.

As our mouths continue to play, my heart threatens to burst out of my chest.

We break our kiss and he places his hands on the sides of my face, his thumbs rubbing my cheeks. "Shelby. Beautiful Shelby."

"Court. Handsome, adorable Court."

He smiles. "No one has ever called me adorable except for Mom."

"Well, now I have."

He cups my face with his hands. "I like it. Hang out with me tomorrow? And the next day? And the next day?" he adds, kissing me on the tip of my nose. His fingers gently trace from my temple all the way down my neck.

"What will Mrs. Stratton say?"

"I say she'll be happy with a few days off."

"Days off?"

"Yes, when she arrives tomorrow I'll tell her she's off until Monday. With pay."

"She's going to be so mad at me."

"You? Why?"

"She loves her job. And she'll think I'm the reason she's getting a paid vacation. A vacation she doesn't want to take."

"She's a smart lady. She'll enjoy her vacation."

I'm thinking I'm going to enjoy her vacation. "If you say so."

"I do. And this will give you a chance to cook me some fried chicken."

Putting my hand on my heart, I feign surprise. "The true reason has come out." I move my hand to his stomach. "It has nothing to do with my kisses and everything to do with your stomach."

"Shelby." His hand covers mine. "I'll take your kisses over your chicken any day of the week."

He pulls me into another mind-blowing kiss, making me forget about Mrs. Stratton, her reaction and fried chicken.

MASQUERADE

LIKE I PREDICTED, Mrs. Stratton isn't happy with her days off. She mumbles something about her husband being home and how she needs her time away.

"Go on a mini-vacation," Court says as she's digging her keys out of her purse. "By yourself. My treat. Charge everything and give me the bill."

"Thanks, but I'll stay home. I'll be back Monday morning. Unless you decide you want to give me more time off."

"Monday it is." Court walks with her down the hall, to the garage where he lets her park her car while she's here.

I've run, showered and found myself putting on a little extra make-up this morning. I almost broke out the false eye lashes, but decided that would be going a little too far.

Dale always made me wear them when we went out, or had business dinners. Toward the end, he wanted me to wear them to work, but half the time I refused.

I should burn them. But I do like how they make my eyes look.

He walks into the kitchen. "Victory."

I laugh seconds before he gathers me in his arms, kissing me like he's been doing this his whole life.

"All alone, finally." He manages the words between kisses that threaten to make my knees buckle.

Since he made the statement the other night about getting to know me, I don't think his words mean he wants to end up in the bedroom, but I'm wondering how we avoid that if his kisses stay this amazing.

After not near long enough, we stop kissing. "I know last night I said I'd work from home, but I have to go to work to get the work to work from home."

"One more time?"

We both laugh. "Come with me?" he asks.

"Sure. But I need to be back by one o'clock. VBS ends at noon, but Phoebe invited them to stay for lunch."

"We'll be back by then."

We hold hands as we walk toward the hallway that leads to the garage. Before we start down the hall, Court kisses me and I wonder why we are leaving in the first place.

"Do we have to leave?" I ask.

He pushes his hand through his hair. "If we don't this phone is going to start ringing off the hook. I've already received three emails since I started kissing you."

"Okay. Off to work."

We hold hands in his SUV all the way there, riding in silence, the music turned down so low you can't make out the tune, let alone the words.

But I don't mind. The silence is nice for a moment. Lets me process Court and this crazy journey, which has enabled me to forget about my dad and the race that we're going to be at together.

I start to sweat thinking about all those disasters waiting to happen, but I steer my mind away, back to the beautiful feeling of Court's lips on mine.

He pulls into a Chevrolet dealership. "Now you can meet Susan," he says as he opens my door.

"Nice."

Court is very businesslike and totally not kissy-like as we walk into the business he owns. Everyone smiles, some say hello, others just watch.

We head to the right, and I notice a big office with glass all around it. Must be Court's.

A cute, young woman sits at a desk outside his office.

"Hello, Mr. Treyhune," she says as we walk up.

"Hi, Susan." He turns to me. "Shelby, this is Susan. Susan, this is, Shelby."

Susan stands and shakes my hand. "It's nice to meet you," she says. "I've heard a lot of great things about you."

"Thank you. Same here."

As she sits, I notice her gaze lingers a bit long on Court. She's really young. If I had to guess, I would say she was crushing a little on her boss.

But then again, so am I. I just happen to be old enough to handle it.

Maybe.

"I'm putting some things together to work from home for the next couple of days. I'll be back in Monday."

Definitely crushing as I see a disappointed look cross her face. I also see a knowing look as she shifts her gaze between me and Court.

"Has Jared come by today?" Court asks.

"I haven't seen him. Is he supposed to?"

"Not sure. I'll touch base with him. He's supposed to be gathering some information for me."

"Anything I can help with?" she asks.

"No. Thanks, though. But there has been a change in plans. The big Fourth of July event we are sponsoring? I need you to take all that over. I have to be out of town that weekend. No way around it. I wish there were. Can you handle everything for the event?"

"I can. How is your dad doing?"

"He's doing well enough to order me around."

She gives Court a thumbs up. "Glad to hear he's better. Can't keep Cal down for long."

The way she says Cal is like she's a friend of the family. I don't think I'd ever feel that comfortable around any of the Treyhunes. I'll have to remember to ask Court how long Susan has been working for him.

Court has disappeared into his office leaving me standing awkwardly in the outer office with Susan.

Susan with a crush on Court.

Susan's phone rings, and I take a step back. No need for me to be in her conversation zone.

It becomes clear quickly though that it is Jared who is on the other line. Susan is lighthearted with him just like she is with Court.

Flirty, even.

Court steps out of his office, then shuts the door. He holds his key up and she nods her head and mouths, "I have a key."

Court nods then leans his head toward the door, indicating he is ready to leave.

"Yes, Jared. Court's here. But he's going to work—"

Before she can finish her sentence, Court is slicing his finger across his throat telling her to stop her part of the conversation.

"He's going to work…really hard today."

Court nods again and she gives him the thumbs up again while mouthing the words, "I've got you covered."

I can see the relief on Court's face, and I wonder how strained the relationship is between Court and Jared.

And how much my presence has added to the strain.

AS WE REACH the car, Court stashes his work in the trunk.

"You might forget it if you put it in there," I say.

"That's the point."

Court starts the car. "We aren't working when we get back. There'll be plenty of time for that this afternoon. No, we are going swimming."

Swimming? Oh.

While I like the thought of seeing Court in his trunks, I don't like the thought of him seeing my lack-of-sun white body in a bathing suit.

A bathing suit that I didn't bring.

Feeling totally off the hook I say, "I'd love to swim, but I didn't bring a suit. But, I'll throw on a pair of shorts and sit at the water's edge while you swim."

"No suit?"

His expression indicates how surprised he is.

"Hey, I came to Florida to work, not bask in the sun."

"I guess you thought I would be a real pain. Not even a day off to enjoy the beaches, huh?"

I'm not going into my mental state as I was packing for this venture. Swimming and beaches were the last thing on my mind as I shoved miscellaneous items in the suitcase.

Ugly items as Bristol indicated.

Court takes a left where he should have taken a right to go to the house. I point in the direction we were supposed to turn. "You made a wrong turn."

"No I didn't."

"I'm confused. Where are we going?"

"To buy you a swimsuit. I'm buying. This will be fun."

My face heats at the thought. "No. That's okay. You don't need to. I have money, but other than the short time I'm here, I'm not going to need a suit, so let's skip it."

He smiles. "Not on your life. There's a touristy place right down here. They sell all kinds of suits."

"A touristy place? That will be expensive."

"I'll never spend all my money. Let me buy you bathing suit. Please?"

Knowing that no matter how long I talk, I'm not going to talk Court out of this, I resign myself to the fact that he's going to purchase a swimsuit for me. I just need to go in, grab the first thing I see that isn't revealing, then we'll be done.

When we enter the store, two very young, very cute sales girls greet us with smiles and spray tans. "Hi. Can we be of assistance today?"

"No" flies out of my mouth while "yes" flies out of Court's. "I need one of you to help my friend with the purchase of a bathing suit," he says, winning the battle of the differing answers.

The blonde chick flashes her smile and winks at Court. Brazen! "I'll be happy to assist you guys. What type of suit are you looking for," she asks Court.

"The suit is for me." I direct her attention away from Court.

"I know."

She switches her focus back to Court.

"Whatever the lady wants." He nods toward me.

"Where are your one pieces?" I ask.

"One pieces?" Court and the sales associate speak at the same time.

"There's the exception." Court shakes his head. "I'm not paying for a one piece."

I stand, crossing my arms. "You don't have to. I will."

There. That will show him. I really don't want him buying me a suit.

The sales girl is looking strangely at me. "We only have a few one pieces over in the corner. You can go down the street to the women's shop. They have a much bigger selection."

Court is still shaking his head. "We're not going down the street. We're buying here."

"Fine," I say. "But I think I can pick out my own suit." I start to head to the one-piece corner, but Court stops me.

He places a kiss on my cheek. "I'm sure you can, but I want to help."

Even though I'm warmed by his kiss, I stand by my resolve. "Look, I don't need any more skin than necessary exposed to the sun. I've been too busy working to have any beach time the last few years."

"I'm sure they sell great sunscreen here."

"We do. It's very expensive." The sales lady's tone is harsh after witnessing Court's kiss to my cheek.

It now matches her narrowed eyes and slightly less enthusiastic nature.

"One piece." It's all I say as Court follows me to that section of the store.

I grab a pretty coral-colored suit.

Court holds his finger up, stopping me from heading into the fitting room. He starts looking at the suits, the noise of the hangers sliding across the rod indicating he doesn't see anything he likes.

The sliding noise stops and he hands me a red suit. "Even though this suit is red, it's my white flag. I surrender."

After trying the suits on, I step out of the dressing room.

"Well?" he asks.

"The red one is nice. I like it."

"But you like the coral one better," he replies.

"No. I don't. The red one it is."

He tries to grab it out of my hand. "Come on, Shelby. Let me buy you a bathing suit. I'm the one forcing you to go swimming."

Years of independence hold on to the suit. "I am capable of paying for it. And I will."

"Women."

It's all he says but he doesn't argue anymore. After I pay for the suit, he picks up a couple of sunscreens with different SPF's. "This should keep your skin fair. Unlike that practically non-SPF sunscreen Jared bought for you."

I love how he casually disses his best friend. "Thank you." My answer is short as is usual when I'm not in a good mood. The last thing I want to do is go to Court's house and put on this bathing suit and swim. Alone.

With Court.

At least the girls will come home at one.

We aren't in the car five minutes when Court's phone buzzes. He answers and it is Jenny asking if the girls can stay and swim in the afternoon when they are finished with their lunch.

They agree Teresa will come over when we return home and get the girls' bathing suits.

"Maybe we should go over there and join them," I say, trying to figure out how I'm going to handle the afternoon.

"Can you say cannon balls and Marco Polo? I don't think so."

"I love those games. And I can land a mean cannon ball. You better watch out."

I say those words to him, but my heart is saying them to myself.

When in actuality, I'm the one who better watch out before I become caught in my own masquerade.

MISGIVINGS

I DON'T KNOW WHAT I was picturing when I imagined Court in swimming attire, but I couldn't imagine and picture anything close to how he looks.

Trim, fit, a little base tan.

Whoo. My suit looks okay, but my body is pale.

"I like the suit," he says as he retrieves a couple of balls out of a storage area next to the pool. I would bet money his mouth opened a little too far when he saw me.

And my money would be on the fact that my ghost-like appearance has caused his jaw to drop.

He tosses the beach balls into the pool and walks toward me. When he reaches me he runs his index finger down my arm. "I like your skin. It's soft. Beautiful. I see why you don't get in the sun."

"I'm not a sun hater. I love being in the sun. It's just working six or seven days a week from sunup until sundown doesn't give a girl much chance to play."

"Come here. Have a seat."

We walk to one of the lounge chairs. I sit next to him, loving the warm feel of the sun on my skin.

Court grabs a bottle of the sunscreen he bought. I hold out my hand and he shakes his head. "My turn."

As he squeezes the coconut smelling lotion on his hand, I breathe with anticipation of his touch. He starts on my shoulders and back. While the lotion is cool, it doesn't stay that way long as his strong hand rubs my skin gently.

"So, why'd you work so hard all the time? Pretty lady like you should have been out having fun."

This is where I have to be careful. I don't want to say too much, yet

139

too little can arouse one's suspicions just as much. "I was with a start-up company. And you know how business is. It takes hard work to make it in these times."

"Was it your company?"

"No."

"According to Barb your whole situation was tough. I know you had a vested interest. I wish I could say I was sorry it didn't work out. But I'm not. Otherwise you wouldn't be here."

His warm touch doesn't stop the chills forming on my arms at his words. Court is smart. It's not surprising, but this isn't the conversation I expected we'd have at the pool. I don't want to talk about Dale and the broken engagement. I don't want that to ever enter my world here.

"It's the guy Barb told me about, isn't it?"

I knew he would put it together. "Yes."

"That's a bad scene. I think I'm headed for something like that at TAG."

I know he just said something about his work, but he's worked his way to my arms, and I'm determined he's not touching my legs. "As much as I like your touch, I'll handle below the belt line."

He laughs and squirts some lotion onto my open palm.

"I think Jared's embezzling."

I stop rubbing and look at him. "Jared?"

He sets the bottle down, and I quickly smooth the rest of the lotion onto my legs, not caring if I miss spots.

"Yes. I don't want to believe it, but all signs are pointing to him."

"Could someone be setting him up?"

"I'm looking into it. It's just that Jared doesn't have the best track record with me, so that makes it harder. He's taken things that belong to me before."

"Yet he's still your best friend?"

"Yes. He's had his problems in the past, but I thought they were resolved. Now with all these money issues he's having, I'm afraid he's taken a route he didn't intend to take. He probably felt trapped."

I scan the parameter of the house. Mansion. "Couldn't he have come to you if he needed money?"

"Yes. He could have, but he won't. He never has. He's always done things on the sly, but I always find out about them. You'd think after all these years he would have learned that these things catch up to you eventually."

"Do you have proof?"

It seems such a shame to be wasting a great new suit on a conversation about embezzlement.

"I'm working on it."

I study my fingernails. I know what betrayal from someone close feels like. Dale's betrayal was different, but it was still betrayal.

"You're the first person I feel like I can talk to about this." His hand brushes my arm. "About anything. Everything."

I feel a kiss coming on, so I turn and face Court. His lips meet mine before I can breathe.

I try to keep my mind off Court's Jared confession as we toss the beach ball around in the pool. We've laid out, put more lotion on each other, stolen a couple of kisses and basically just played the afternoon away. Theresa said the girls would be home by four, which is in less than an hour.

"I need to go and shower before the girls come home." I spike the ball once more Court's way before walking up the pool steps.

"I'll go with you."

I turn toward him. Sure we've shared a few kisses, but that doesn't mean we are sharing a shower. "I don't think so."

"I meant I'm going in, too. You go your way, I'll go mine."

Relief runs through me. I would hate to turn this man down for anything, yet I would be turning him down.

I've just finished drying my hair when I hear the girls coming through the front door. I head that way, and it doesn't take me long to find them.

"We had so much fun, Shelby." They wrap their arms around me, hugging me tightly.

I embrace them. "That's great. You got along good with Phoebe?"

"She's a lot of fun. Even if she can't see. She's going to be our best friend. We asked her if she wanted to come spend the night one night, and she said yes. So you have to talk to her mother."

"I will. You guys had a busy day. And you have another one tomorrow."

They hand me a plastic bag. "Here're our bathing suits. They're all wet."

"That's okay. I'll hang them up with mine in my bathroom."

The look on Team Twin's face can only be described as confused. "You went swimming today?"

I realize they don't know their father is home. They have no idea I've been frolicking in the pool with their dad all afternoon. Kissing their dad.

My face is turning red, and I'm sure they're going to notice. Team Twin doesn't miss much.

"I may have taken a little break and went in the pool for a swim. Is that okay?"

Like I need their permission. The question is more rhetorical, but they don't know that.

"Sure. I guess," Bristol says. "Why don't you go swimming with us?"

I can't reveal I didn't even have a bathing suit until late this morning when their father insisted I buy one. "There hasn't been a whole lot of time for swimming. But maybe we'll have more time now."

"Girls."

At the sound of Court's voice, Team Twin ditches me and runs to Court. He picks them both up in hug and kisses them each on the cheek before setting them back down.

"What are you doing here, Daddy? It's daytime. It's not even dinnertime yet."

"I decided I was working too hard and wanted to come home and surprise my girls. Did you have fun?"

"We did." Team Twin spends the next few minutes telling Court about Bible school, then swimming with Phoebe. "And, we even asked her if she wanted to spend the night with us. Can she soon, please?"

"Of course she can. We'll arrange it."

"Yeah!"

Bristol and Darling high five each other.

"Where would you girls like to go for dinner?" he asks, looking them, then at me.

"FunTime Burgers. Can we please?" Bristol hugs Darling after she asks.

"I don't see why not," Court says. "Shelby, is that okay with you?"

I look down at the girls and see the dejected look on their face. It only lasts a couple of seconds, but it was there. They thought they were having a night out with their dad.

Court is only looking at me.

"You know," I start. "I think I'll pass. I'm feeling tired after my day, and I'm going to lie down. You guys go and have fun."

Now I have to face the dejected look on Court's face.

"Come on, Shelby. It'll be fun."

Team Twin is staring at me. Not giving in one way or another. No smiles, no frowns. Just straight-line lips and flat eyes.

"Maybe next time."

Before Court can respond, I walk to my room and shut the door. I lean against it and am surprised that I'm blinking back tears. Tears for what?

Court and I aren't an item. We're a summer kissing fling while it lasts. He's got too many issues to contend with right now, and he doesn't even know who I am.

Not his fault, I know, but it's still a fact.

A soft knock raps on my door. I can tell by the height of the knock it's Court and not Bristol or Darling.

I take in a deep breath, and push back those threatening tears of self-pity. Turning, I open the door barely a crack. "Yes?"

I try to make my voice playful.

"Can I come in for a minute?"

Even though I knew he was going to ask, I don't have a good reason why he can't. So I let him in.

He pushes the door shut. "I'm confused here. I see through your act, I just don't know why you said you were tired."

For once I need to be honest. "When you asked me about going, I saw some disappointment in the girls. They thought they were going to have you to themselves for an evening."

He straightens. "Are you sure you aren't seeing things? The girls love having you around."

"I agree. They do like me, but they need to spend some time with you. Just you."

He runs his hand through his hair. "As much as I don't like it, I'll go along with you for tonight. But just tonight. They have to learn to share me sometime."

Share you with who, I want to ask. That random somebody who will come into his life one day? "They will. It's a process."

He kisses me quickly on the nose. "Thank you."

As he leaves the room sadness falls on me again. But I need to become used to it. Everything here is temporary.

Everything.

I DIG THROUGH THE freezer and find a tub of ice cream. Chocolate, my favorite. I locate an ice cream scoop and scoop a nice portion into a bowl. I barely take two bites when the doorbell rings.

Court and the girls have only been gone about thirty minutes, so I'm sure it's not them. Not that they would use the front door anyway.

I look through the peep hole and my stomach sinks.

Jared.

Jared who is possibly embezzling from his best friend and has a track record of other issues which Court has forgiven.

Yet still trusts him with his business.

I don't get it.

Opening the door I paste a smile on my face. "Hello."

"Hi," he says, gently pushing his way into the house. "How's the most beautiful girl in the world tonight?"

"I'm not sure. Why don't you find her and ask her? Your flattery is unbelievable at times." I speak my words lightly and with a smile, but I think he knows I'm serious.

"It's all about perception, Shelby. And right now I perceive you to be that girl. Take a compliment. Say thank you."

I find myself almost taken in by his playful tone, good looks and easy demeanor. He walks into a place and it's instantly a party-type atmosphere.

We head into the kitchen. He spies my bowl of ice cream. "Dessert?"

"Dinner." I instantly regret my words.

Instantly.

Because I know how this man thinks. In less than a few seconds he will ask me out to dinner.

Which I will refuse.

"Come on. A pretty gal like you shouldn't be eating alone. Let me take you out."

I so know his type.

And if my mind wasn't burning with the visions of Court Treyhune I might consider.

Oh, and if Jared wasn't an embezzler.

I wonder if I can help Court. Maybe I can pick Jared's brain and see what he's really up to?

Maybe dinner isn't such a bad idea?

"You've convinced me." I put the bowl of ice cream in the freezer, spoon and all. "Let me grab my purse and we can leave."

Jared has such an I've-won expression on his face.

If he only knew.

MANIPULATE

JARED TAKES ME to an upscale bistro not far from Court's house.

I wonder who is going to pay.

There are no prices on the menu, it's in French, and after I order I wonder what I'm going to be eating. It should be interesting.

Having no idea the easiest way to ask a man if he's an embezzler, I let the conversation flow naturally, but I listen for an opening that might segue into me learning something that could help Court.

The man I'd rather be out to dinner with.

"I think it's cool that you and Court have been friends for so long." Maybe digging into the past will reveal useful information.

"Since we were kids. Playing in the dirt and driving go-karts. That's how we spent our days."

"Did you ever race?"

It's a good thing I was staring at him or I would have missed that look that flashed in his eyes. Resentment? Regret? It was hard to tell, but it wasn't good.

"No. Although I will say I was pretty good at it. Beat Court four out of five times when we raced those go-karts. Never had the money to go into it, though. It's not a cheap sport. And you have to know the right people."

I raise my eyebrows. "You certainly knew the right people."

He twists his wine glass stem, swirling his wine. "I did. But Court was good, too."

What he doesn't say is sinking in. "So Court got the chance to drive, and you didn't."

He shrugs. "Court was Cal's son. Of course they were going to give him the ride. I never expected anything else."

Does he mean the words he's speaking? He sounds sincere, but I have the feeling Jared James can sound however he wants.

He's that kind of guy.

Our salads arrive and I find that I've ordered one I like. The dressing is sweet and sour, reminding me of the man I'm dining with. Our conversation slows while we eat, and I try to study Jared. He garners looks from every female, but I'm sure he's used to that. I wonder at the ladies he dates? Do they ever become used to their date being the recipient of such looks?

I'm sure the girls that date Court have the same issue. Except Court seems more attentive.

Sincerely attentive.

Jared can appear to be attentive.

I really want to ask about his relationship with MaryLeigh. Although that has nothing to do with the embezzling aspect, it's still a part of his relationship with Court. A part Jared felt like he needed to hide for some reason.

And if Jared and Court were such close childhood friends, how is it that Court didn't know MaryLeigh?

This whole triangle is a mystery.

"How did you end up being a nanny?" Jared asks.

I put my fork down. "You ask that question like I've got the plague."

He chuckles. "I'm sorry if it came out like that. Like I said when I first met you don't really seem like nanny material."

Did he just diss me? "I'm not sure what you consider nanny material, but I'm a pretty good one," I say with as much authority as one can use after being a nanny for a short time.

"You take offense for no reason. I think nanny, I think old lady. That's all."

"You need to think again and quit stereotyping." How did the conversation become about me. This is not the way the evening is supposed to be going.

"Believe me, after tonight I will." He winks at me which chills me more than thrills me.

The waiter whisks away our salad plates and in moments our entrees are set before us. My blackened tuna looks good and smells good.

I hope it tastes good.

After one bite I think I might be in heaven.

The tuna takes my mind off the reason I am here. I savor a couple more succulent bites before reeling my mind back to the task at hand.

"There are a couple of people from my childhood that I wish I would have stayed in touch with. You and Court are lucky to have all that history."

Jared takes another sip of his wine. "We are. It's good to know you have a friend that has your back, you know. Through thick and thin as they say."

According to Court there have been a lot of thin times. "Have you guys ever had a falling out?"

Jared's fork halts slightly before resuming its course to his mouth. He chews slowly, thoughtfully probably, before answering. "A couple."

"I bet they were about girls, huh. That's what most guys fight about."

He sets his fork on his plate and wipes his mouth. "You know, if I knew you were going to talk about Court all night, I might have rescinded my invitation."

My face heats at his words. Then I realize this might be a good thing. I didn't want him noticing that I was trying to glean information out of him about him. He thinks I want information about Court.

Maybe I can manipulate this situation to my favor. Although we aren't anywhere near talking about how or why he would be embezzling. But maybe there are underlying issues that would lead to that information if I can find them out.

I smile what I think is my best smile and try to defuse any suspicions Jared might be having. "I'm sorry. I'm curious about him, that's all. I didn't realize that would bother somebody like you."

"Somebody like me?"

"Yes. Smart, too good looking for their own good, every woman's dream date."

With each compliment he puffs up more and more until his smile is wide. He couldn't be sitting any straighter in his chair. "Court's a good guy. I didn't mean to sound jealous or anything. And I need to remember, you're his nanny. Not his girlfriend."

Kisses in the sun, hands rubbing coconut-scented lotion on my body bring Court into my mind. Not that he ever left. But Jared is right.

I'm not his girlfriend.

I'm only his nanny.

Whose job will be done in a couple of months.

But I still can't make myself interested in Jared in the way he wants me to be interested. Especially with the dark clouds of mistrust surrounding him.

We finish eating in silence and when the waitress brings the bill, Jared whips out his card.

I wonder if it will go through.

When the waitress returns, all smiles and flirty, I know the card went through and now she's vying for a big tip.

If her tip is half as big and flamboyant as his signature, she should be very happy.

I'm simply happy the card went through and I don't have to pay.

I KEPT A CLOSE EYE on my watch, but still arrived home later than I wanted to. I knew Court would already be back with the girls, and I'm not sure how the fact that I was out with Jared will go over.

Until I get Court alone and explain, things will be awkward.

Awkward and hostile, it turns out.

I thought I'd seen Court's eyes hard and dark before, but I'd never seen anything like his eyes when I walked in with Jared.

As soon as I hit the kitchen, Court is on his way to me, only to stop short when Jared appears.

His gaze speaks a million words, none of which I want to be the recipient of. I try to converse back with mine, but his gaze shifts to Jared at this point.

Daggers. That word describes the look Court is giving him.

Jared backs up a couple of steps, hands in the air. "Hey. Don't shoot. I just took your nanny out for dinner. She's fine."

I look at Court, trying convey with my eyes what I can't with my words. "Sorry I didn't leave a note or anything. I thought I'd be back before you and the girls came home."

"I guess I distracted her. Made her forget about the time." Jared places his hand on my shoulder and I stop short of cringing. This situation is way out of control.

What led me to believe I could control it in the first place?

Certainly I don't have the best track record with men, so managing two of them, especially two of them that harbor their own dangerous level of hostility toward each other, is no doubt a crazy idea.

Two steps. That's how far away Court is physically, but I can see we are emotionally further apart. Since Jared is behind me a little, and I have Court's attention, I bravely mouth the words, "I can explain."

His eyes soften slightly, but only slightly. They almost seem to say "I'm not sure any explanation will suffice."

Unlike the other night where Court said nothing to Jared about leaving, tonight he's taking another route.

"Since it's after ten, the girls are asleep," Court says. "Which is a perfect time to go over some things with Shelby."

Court starts walking to the foyer, and Jared gets the picture that he's being asked to leave.

"Until Friday night," he says to me, winking. "I'm looking forward to it."

His expression begs a similar response, but I can't. The playful act I used earlier won't fly now. "I'll see you then."

He looks a little hurt but doesn't say anything. As soon as the door shuts, Court twists the lock and turns to me.

"I thought you might have gone for a run. Did you even look at your phone? I called. I was worried."

I swallow hard. Not expecting any calls, my phone still lies buried in my purse. "I didn't look at my phone. But I can explain."

Court leans against the heavy, ornate door. "It was like a knife plunged into my heart when I saw you walk in with him."

My knees threaten to buckle at his words. What has taken place that these strong words come out of his mouth? "I can explain. It is not what you're thinking."

He shakes his head and pushes off the door. "Funny. Those are the same words MaryLeigh spoke."

MEND

MY BREATH HITCHES. "MaryLeigh?"

He stands now in the middle of the foyer, the chandelier casting shadows on the walls, and light on his face. "Yes. MaryLeigh."

"I was only trying to help you."

He laughs, but it's not a jovial laugh. "Help me?"

"Yes." Not wanting to see Court in any more turmoil I walk to him, leaving only inches between us.

I have no idea why I want to mend his hurt, but I do. I touch his face, my thumb rubbing his cheek, while my fingers play with the hair at the nape of his neck. "He accused me of going out with him to find out information about you."

"Did you succeed?" His voice is husky, and I wonder how much my touch has to do with that.

"I had to back off once he found me out." I smile hoping my words ease his soul.

"Then what did you talk about?"

His voice is a whisper, and it's a good thing we are so close or I might not have heard him. "Different things. I wanted to find out if he is embezzling from you."

His lips are a straight line and stay that way. "How did you think you were going to find that out? Just ask him?"

"No, silly. But the more I hang out with him, get comfortable with him, you never know what might slip."

"It's too dangerous."

"Dangerous?"

"I don't want you falling for him."

"How can I when I've already fallen for you."

And I have fallen.

Hard.

Court won't be easy to recover from, but I'm a big girl. I'll be okay in the end, but right now I want to enjoy every aspect of this man and situation.

Every aspect.

I stand on my tiptoes and touch my lips to his. His arms pull me to him, and our kiss bridges any gap that may have been between us.

"Don't scare me like that again, Shelby," he says after our kiss ends.

"I won't." I stand in his arms, feeling like it's the best place on earth.

And right now it is.

"Did you hug him?"

"Just hello."

"You smell like him. I don't like it."

"I'll make sure I shower. Soon."

"Please.

Would now be a good time to broach the subject of MaryLeigh and Jared? There are some things I still don't understand. "Can I ask you a question?"

"Sure."

"It might be a tough one."

"I'm a tough guy."

"Can we go and sit?"

"We can."

We walk to the living room, but this time, instead of sitting opposite each other, we plop down next to each other, practically in each other's lap.

But not quite.

So do I bring up his agenda or mine first? His statement about how MaryLeigh and I spoke the same words is very intriguing, but so is the aspect that Jared and Court grew up together and were apparently close, yet Jared knew MaryLeigh and Court didn't.

I'll start with my agenda.

One might naturally lead into the other.

He takes my hand in his, and it feels like we've been doing this forever. I like it. I like how his touch makes me feel.

"You said that Jared and MaryLeigh knew each other from childhood. You and Jared were pretty tight growing up. How is it you didn't know

MaryLeigh, too?"

"They hid her from me."

"Hid her? Like in a closet or something?"

His thumb rubs my fingers, making it hard to concentrate on anything but our touch.

But I have to.

"First I have to say that I'm not sure what the truth is. They both had a story. Similar but not entirely matching. But over time details can get blurry. At least that's what they told me."

"That and the same people can see the same incident, yet have totally different aspects of what happened."

"True. The story is that MaryLeigh knew who I was, but she was embarrassed about her upbringing. She lived in a tenement in the city. A pretty rough neighborhood. Jared and she were friends, and she made him promise not to say anything about her or introduce her until she could better her situation."

To voice the words "that is the silliest thing I've ever heard" would be so hypocritical. But I should say something. "How did she better her situation?"

"Those details are fuzzy. I've never been told. But when Jared did introduce her, he acted like he just met her at a club. She lived in a very nice apartment in the best part of town. She dressed impeccably and had it all together."

I hope he doesn't notice that I can't look him in the eye. Every word he speaks is like hammering the proverbial nail in my coffin. "Was it love at first sight?"

He laughs. "She says it was, but she had been seeing me for years by then and I didn't know. It was a fast courtship and we were married in less than two months. The twins came along one year later, almost on our anniversary."

"So when did you find out about Jared and MaryLeigh?" The look on his face makes me add, "Their friendship. That's all it was, right?"

"So they say. Those words you said, 'It's not what you're thinking' are the same words MaryLeigh used to tell me when I would ask her about Jared."

"You do believe them, don't you?"

"I wish I could. There's so much you don't know about. I think MaryLeigh was always taken with him, but my money and fame were more important."

That's how it was. No wonder he's so hurt and sensitive where Jared is concerned.

I look at him and wonder how anyone could not love this man. Be with him, marry him, simply for who he is. Impossible. "I'm sure she loved you."

"I'm not as sure as you are."

"You stayed married."

"I stayed rich."

Part of me wonders how cynical Court is. I'm sure anyone in his position in life would have reason to be somewhat cynical, but would they have to live that way all their life in every aspect?

He releases my hand and runs his fingers through my hair. "That's why I'm so taken with you. I know you are running from something, but you weren't running to something. Like me. I can trust who you are, Shelby. That is the most important thing."

Tell him.

Tell him now.

Tell him how you grew up living in a trailer park. How you got made fun of all your school days. How the boy with the wealthiest parents noticed you, and when you gave him what he wanted, he joined the crowd who snubbed you and made fun of you at school going down the hall.

"Thank you for being real. I don't think I can take any more people who aren't who they say they are. I'm through."

He pulls me to him and kisses me until it is impossible to think of speaking.

Or to think about the childhood I'm hiding.

THURSDAY AND Friday pass quickly with Court working for a couple of hours each morning, then we would have a late morning swim, indulge in a kiss or two, get the girls from next door and head out for an afternoon of fun.

We didn't talk about Jared or the upcoming Rolling Stones concert I was going to with him in just a few short hours from now.

Three to be exact.

He's picking me up at six.

Court has been brooding all day. Even Team Twin notice and ask him what is wrong.

No matter how many times I tell him it is a fact finding mission, he chooses to ignore me.

The girls are swinging at the park, and Court and I are sitting on a bench under the shade of a tree.

I tap him on the shoulder. "I can't stand the thought of you being mad at me."

"I'm not mad." He clenches his fists as he speaks.

"Maybe not mad, but you're something."

"What guy wouldn't be something knowing his girl is going out with his best friend?"

"It's not a date."

"I've said it before. That's how you see it. It's not how he sees it."

"He will. There will be nothing happening but me singing along with Mick Jagger. Besides, I'm going to keep digging. You have to settle that embezzlement issue. That has to be weighing on you."

He looks at me and actually scoots a little away from me. "Have you ever thought I may not really want to solve it?"

"Seriously? Why not?"

"What if I don't want it to be true?"

"I'm sure you don't want it to be true. But it appears somebody is taking your hard-earned money. It needs to stop."

"This whole situation stinks."

"It does. But think of how good it will feel to have everything out in the open. You'll feel better."

"You already make me feel better. Isn't that enough?"

As much as I'm flattered by his attention, I'm anxious about every other aspect of our togetherness. "I know it's hard. But the right thing has to be done."

"I'm going to blow your phone up with texts all night."

"So juvenile."

"That's how I feel. Like I'm back in all the high school mess. Girl, guy, other guy wanting girl."

I laugh. "Now you sound like a caveman."

"Me Tarzan—"

"Stop," I say, as I try to control my laughter. I'm glad something is making me laugh. Our conversation from a couple of nights ago has been weighing heavily on my mind.

I've envisioned several scenarios where I blurt out, "I was raised in a trailer park. But my parents were kind and loving. Still are. You want to meet them July fourth?"

Then every bit of my insides cringe, and I think that I'm acting crazy and that he really won't care if I was raised in a trailer park and he would probably love my parents.

It's me that's uncomfortable with the situation. I realize I'm pretty much acting like he is. Twice burned…and that whole thing. I keep telling myself Court isn't Paul or Dale. Court's not going to say see you later.

Court hasn't attempted to do anything but kiss me. But that's how Paul was at first.

Then there was Dale. Giving that man everything I had and then some things I didn't know I had, all to be dumped.

For an heiress.

Dale didn't draw lines when it came to status and background and professions. At least that's what he said.

And we shouldn't. We are all the same. Every one of us breathes in and out.

But sometimes the air we breathe in and out is different.

Too different in some cases.

.

MOVE

MICK JAGGER IS everything I thought he'd be and more. He's still a wild-child on stage, and the arena is screaming with voices singing along to all the best songs.

Jared is acting like a perfect gentleman. I have no reason to complain. He hasn't attempted to do anything inappropriate. I hope I've been right all along and Court has been wrong in his assessment of the situation.

My ears are still ringing as we leave the show. It's almost eleven o'clock and I am starving, but I'm not saying anything to Jared. The sooner he takes me home the better.

I answered the first couple of texts from Court, but then, especially considering nothing was happening I told him I'd text him when I was on the way back to the house.

Jared helps me into his car, always the gentleman.

"Do you feel like grabbing something to eat? There's a lot of great diners around here. I'm sorry we didn't get to eat before the concert. I had no idea every place would be so crowded."

My stomach says yes, but my heart says no.

Jared looks disappointed as I turn down his offer, but he doesn't complain or try and talk me into going. The more I think about the evening, the more I realize Jared hasn't been his usual self tonight.

"Thanks for taking me. I have always wanted to see Mick Jagger. One thing off my bucket list."

He chuckles as we sit in the long line of traffic waiting to exit the deck. "You're too young to have a bucket list."

"I didn't think there was an age limit."

"I think old people make bucket lists."

"I guess you don't have one."

"Not quite. Besides, I think I've done almost everything I've ever dreamed of doing. Except getting married and having a family. Other than that, I've been knocking out my dreams left and right. It's been great."

I wonder what'll happen when the dreams turn into nightmares. Or maybe they already have and that's where he found himself in trouble.

And I'm assuming he's in trouble. Because Court is assuming as much.

I decide to run with what little information he provided a moment ago. "You're ready to be married?"

"If I find the right girl. She's been eluding me."

I'm hoping the she he's referring to is an ambiguous she and I'm not she. Now I'm not anxious to continue with this conversation. "I guess getting married and having kids are a natural ambition for most people."

"What about you?"

He's not going to be the recipient of the broken engagement story. "Maybe someday. But I'm content for now."

"Content taking care of someone else's kids."

"It's a good break for me. I'm enjoying it."

What I'm enjoying more than taking care of the kids is kissing their father. I blush at the thought and am glad it's dark. Jared is very observant, and not a lot of things escape his notice.

He would have noticed the blush.

"My assistant is pregnant. She's about to have her baby anytime now."

I remember Court mentioning that. Why is Jared mentioning it? "That's nice. Boy? Girl?"

"She doesn't know. She wants it to be a surprise."

"That's fun. You don't hear of that too much anymore. Obviously she and her husband agreed to wait to find out."

"She's not married."

"Oh."

He laughs. "It's okay. She's good with everything. I thought for a while she would have a rough time of it, but I guess her parents came through and bailed her out of some stuff financially, so she's all ready for the baby."

"That's good. I imagine it's tough enough adjusting to having a new baby, I can't imagine having financial worries on top of that."

Financial worries.

I look at Jared who's looking straight ahead, preventing me from seeing his eyes and facial expressions. "She's lucky to have such generous parents."

I hope I don't emphasize the words parents.

And I hope it was indeed her parents that helped her out of that financial jam and not Jared James.

I DECIDE TO VOICE MY concerns to Court once Jared has left. Again, he was quick to take the hint and leave, and he was barely out of the driveway before I broached the subject with Court.

Court listens intently. When I'm done retelling the story, he shrugs his shoulders. "Could be. I can't figure out what he's spending his money on. At least this scenario makes sense."

"Well, we don't know if it's true or not. We're speculating. But it's something to look into. How well does Susan know Jared's assistant?"

"I'm not sure. I can find out though."

I pick up the invitation Team Twin made for the vacation Bible school program on Sunday morning. They also made one for Uncle Jared. "Do you think Jared will come Sunday morning?"

"I don't know. He does love those girls."

I sense sadness in his voice as well as in his gaze. "This whole thing has you torn up inside, doesn't it."

"There are a lot of things that have me feeling a bit discombobulated." I'm hoping I'm one of those things. He has yet to kiss me tonight, or even make a move toward me like he is going to kiss me.

In fact, he is keeping his distance, which is something he hasn't done since we shared that first kiss.

I sniff my shirt.

"What are you doing?" he asks.

"Seeing if I smell like Jared. You're awfully far away from me and not making any moves to be closer."

"It's not intentional. I promise. I have a lot on my mind tonight."

He reaches his hand out and I take his in mine. Neither of us move closer to the other. Hand in hand is satisfying right now. It's a connection.

One that I'm finding harder and harder to break as each day goes by.

And I'm going to be miserable when that breaking day does come.

MELTING

SUNDAY MORNING IS chaos as I try and ready the girls for their program. And I need to get ready myself. As much as the girls insist I don't have to dress up, they both seem to forget that's all I brought. Work clothes, running clothes and not much in between.

Jared does show up and it's an awkward group that walks next door to the church that takes place in a house.

Court is screaming handsome this morning, and I'm hoping there are no single females at this church. And if there are I hope they latch onto Jared and leave Court alone.

Nice thoughts to go to church with. Keeping your man to yourself.

And trying to rid yourself of another one.

Team Twin are bursting at the seams and run down the hall when we step into the house.

Knowing no better, Court, Jared and I follow them. When we do enter the room, I discover there are plenty of people here. I don't know what I was expecting, but this crowd wasn't it.

Jenny and Stephen greet us right away, and we introduce "Uncle Jared" to them.

Several more people come over in the course of the next few minutes, including Stephen's Uncle Roger, the pastor. I haven't felt this welcome in any place but Court's arms recently.

Is it bad to compare church people to embracing a man?

My face heats a little at the thought. It's a good thing no one can read my thoughts.

After a few minutes some people stand up front. Roger plays the guitar and a couple of gals sing. The words are on the wall and I follow along as best as I can. Without knowing the tunes it's hard, but a couple of the songs have upbeat tempos and are somewhat repetitive, so that makes it easier.

After what is referred to as a shortened message, which still took over thirty minutes, the kids take over up front.

Bristol and Darling seem at home with all the other kids. I do notice all the other kids have tamed hair, while Bristol and Darling still sport their wild look. But that battle isn't mine.

The kids put on a skit, which at points has us laughing. They all do a good job of remembering their lines.

They sing and are truly having a great time. Team Twin look like they were made for the stage. Maybe this is what they need.

An audience.

I'm not sure about the homeschooling aspect, not that I've looked into it too much these past few days. But it seems they thrive in this environment surrounded by other kids.

Or maybe it's God they're thriving under.

When the program is over, Bristol and Darling run up to Court. They both start talking at once. "Did you like it, Daddy? Can we come back here next Sunday? They have church here. All the kids come. Can we, please?"

Court seems overwhelmed by their request. I'm not sure where he is with the whole God thing, other than he doesn't have any faith.

I would say I am comfortable here, but it's in an uncomfortable way. It's like my heart's been stirred to come to this place where people celebrate Jesus. I've always viewed church as something I do if I have time.

This group makes me want to make the time.

But I'm not butting in and offering to bring them back. I'll be gone in August so I'm not starting something I can't finish.

I notice Court doesn't commit, instead answering them with a vague "we'll see." But Team Twin seems okay with his answer. They head over to a group of kids, who welcome them in.

I also notice Jared talking to a woman. Very pretty, dark hair. Did I say very pretty?

Roger comes up to Court and me as we stand waiting for the twins to say they are ready to go. I notice Court keeps staring at Jared, and I can't imagine the emotions running through him.

Best friend or foe?

Now armed with the knowledge of Jared's assistant having financial troubles, things might be falling into place. Not a good place, but at least there might be motivation.

"Your daughters had a great time this week," Roger says. "And it's good seeing you here. My wife and I have been praying for all of you. I know the past couple of years haven't been easy."

"No, they haven't," Court agrees.

Roger looks at me. "Bristol and Darling talked about you a lot, Shelby. They really look up to you."

"Oh. That's nice. I'm fairly new."

"We're glad you're here. We certainly hope to see you again, and if there is anything we can do for you, please let us know."

Everyone seems to be lingering, talking in small groups while children are running around. This brings new meaning to the word church. I could come here every week.

Roger steps away to talk to someone else.

"Are you ready?" Court asks.

"Whenever you are. But good luck rounding up Team Twin. I think they would live here if they could. And did you see Jared chatting with that pretty brunette over there?"

I point in the direction of Jared.

"Maybe she'll be his next prey."

Court sounds jaded.

And in light of things, he has reason to sound that way. "We need to figure out what's going on. You can't go along forever suspicious of your best friend."

"I know. But it's how I'm going to feel until we prove otherwise."

An idea starts forming. "Can you get me access to your business bank accounts?"

"Yes. Why?"

"I don't want to go into much detail now, but let me look around your bank accounts for the last few months. Maybe I'll come up with something."

"Here he comes," Court says softly.

"This is a cool place," Jared says when he reaches Court and me. "I really like this church."

I laugh. "You like it because you were talking to a pretty woman. We saw you."

"Well, you can't see past my best friend here and turned me down. It's time to move on. Her name is Stace and her half sister owns the house next door."

"I always knew you were a fast mover." Court tries to lighten his voice. I notice it didn't work, but Jared doesn't catch the seriousness with which Court speaks.

"I learned from the best." Jared smiles at Court before punching him in the upper arm.

"You didn't learn everything from me. By the way, how's Janice doing? Has she had her baby yet?"

"No. Anytime now. I keep checking my phone. She said she'd let me know when she went to the hospital. Why are you asking? Is Susan too bogged down with all the work? I can hire a temp. I don't mind."

"Susan's fine. I was just wondering."

Detective Court. He's not very subtle.

It's a good thing he has me.

IT'S MONDAY morning and Court is back to work.

Mrs. Stratton is back to work.

I'm back to work.

And Team Twin is back to work. Screaming like there's no tomorrow. I mistakenly thought after a few days of vacation Bible school that they would be better behaved, but although they were amazingly good yesterday, today is a different story.

Today Court isn't here.

No fun in the sun with Daddy. Just boring Shelby.

That's what they called me.

Even though I try to do the same things their dad did last week. When he suggests something it's fun and they wouldn't want to do anything else.

But let me suggest the same thing and it's boring.

I'm standing in the doorway to their room trying to figure out what we are going to do this afternoon. I suggested swimming but they said no.

I still want to take a brush or a pair of scissors to their hair. I constantly bite my tongue to keep from saying anything. But at least I know it all stems from MaryLeigh.

MaryLeigh, who I'm still trying to figure out.

Between her and Jared, I don't think Court's had a moment of peace in a long time.

"How about a piggy back ride," Bristol says. "I can jump on your back."

"How about that's a no. You're too heavy."

Bristol stomps her foot. "Uncle Jared gives us piggy back rides."

"The next time you see your Uncle Jared, ask him to give you one. I'm not Uncle Jared."

Bristol looks pensive if that's possible for a ten-year-old. "Uncle Jared is fun. But not as much fun as he used to be. He's different now. He doesn't play as much. He's too busy talking to grown-ups."

"And talking on the phone," Darling adds. "Everybody talks on their phones. When can we have phones? Some of our friends already have them."

They are derailing the subject of Jared. "You'll have to talk to your dad about the phone. And I guess grown-ups do look busy when they are talking or texting. But you guys like to play with your tablets."

"Yeah, but not all the time," Bristol says.

"I bet the next time you see your Uncle Jared he would put his phone away if you asked him. And he'd probably give you a piggy back ride, too."

"Maybe," Bristol says. "We'll see."

I hope Court brings home the access to the bank accounts. The sooner we can get this mess cleared up, the better.

But if Jared is guilty, there will be a huge void in the Treyhune home.

Huge.

MEASURE

IT'S THREE IN the morning and I have been looking over this bank account for the last six hours. Everything seems to be in order. There have been a few high-dollar transactions, but they all look legitimate. Court gave up at midnight, and I told him I wouldn't be too much longer.

The feel of looking at the numbers, trying to make sense of certain figures has brought me back to a place I like to be. A place I'm familiar with.

Forget unbrushed hair and games of Old Maid. This is where I need to be. Yes, I needed to distance myself from Dale and that whole scene, but I haven't thought of Dale in a long time, thanks to Court, and I'm ready to dive back into the financial world.

I will keep my commitment here for the summer, and I'll miss Court when I go back to Atlanta, but I have to go back.

I'll call Barb tomorrow, or today, rather, and have her start putting feelers out to see if anyone is hiring. She and her husband know everybody.

As I'm about to close out another month's transactions, I stop. I scroll back down at the check numbers I just passed by. Six checks in a row all for the same amount.

That's strange. I haven't seen a pattern like this in all the months that I've already scanned through.

When I click on the show image button, I sit straighter in my chair. The check is made out to Rajed Media. That was the name on the checks Court had printed copies of.

I look to my left at the pile of papers, but the checks aren't in the stack. I close that image and click on the next check number. Same payee, same amount, same date. And so on for the next four checks.

Were the checks Court printed out all written the same day? I remember them being the same amount, but the date doesn't ring a bell.

You think he or I would have noticed that.

I print the front of the last check in this sequence. Then I click the button to print the back of the check.

As the image comes up, my pulse quickens and sweat forms on my forehead.

Jared's crazy signature is sprawled across the back of this check. Not wanting to believe what I'm seeing, I print it and quickly click into the previous check.

Same thing. Jared's signature on the back. I print the front and back of each check. When they are all in front of me, I look at the bank information on the back of the check. All the checks were deposited in the same account on the same day.

The bank is a local bank, not a nationwide chain.

I debate whether to wake Court or let him continue to sleep.

The proof that he didn't want to see is right here. I can't imagine how Court is going to feel. Tears threaten and I dab the corners of my eyes. I'm not sure if they are for the truth coming to light or for Court and the betrayal of his best friend.

"What did you find?"

Looking up, I see Court standing in the doorway. "You're still awake?"

"I was dozing, but the sound of the printer made me curious. I guess you've found something."

I push the papers across the desk. He walks over, picks them up and shuffles through them, but he doesn't turn them over.

"These are the same checks I printed out the other day."

"They are. Look at the back. Look who deposited them."

Court's eyebrows raise and his lips purse as he looks at each check one by one. Almost like he's not believing what he's seeing, he shuffles back through the checks, a little slower this time.

He shakes his head from left to right before setting the copies on the desk. "I was right. I can't believe I was right."

Walking around the desk, I fall into Court's arms, hugging him tight, trying to take away his pain. I know it's an impossible task, only time can heal wounds like these, but any measure of comfort is helpful.

I still remember Barb's hug when I was hurting so badly over Dale.

The tears I cried on her shoulder.

It feels like ages ago. So much has changed in my life, I hardly recognize the old one when memories like this surface.

I can't even remember what Dale's touch felt like.

But I can remember the hurt, the pain, and I hate that Court is going through the same thing.

Like I said before, betrayal is betrayal.

It all hurts.

COURT COMES home early the next day, and we take Team Twin to the park. Court and I sit on the same bench we sat on the last time we were here. The girls are constantly fighting with that hair as they play.

But we aren't here to talk about their hair.

"Have you decided what you're going to do?" I ask.

"I went through my personal account because Jared had written me a check a while back, and it was the same account. So there's no doubt he got the money."

"I know you are disappointed."

"Even though it's what I expected all along, I had no idea how much it would affect me. He called me twice today and I didn't answer. I have to talk to him sometime, but knowing is different than expecting. No matter how high your expectations are."

"High? Don't you mean low?"

The agony on Court's face hurts my heart. I'm not sure I've hurt this badly for anyone else before. For me? Yes. This is a strange feeling.

"There's so much involved here," he says. "Not just a friendship, but a business relationship as well. Jared runs my stores. He's taking the burden of that off me. I'll need to replace him."

"Are you going to send him to jail?"

"Jail?"

"This is a felony. We found a few checks that equal a lot of money. What if there's more? He could have been stealing from you for years."

"You could replace him."

His words jar their way through my body. "What?"

"You. You have the background. You are a financial whiz."

I rub my forehead. "You're not thinking right."

167

"Tell me why? This is a job made for you."

I'm flustered beyond belief. The only thing that has kept my sanity is knowing I'd be leaving here in a couple of months. How can I work for this man I've fallen for? "I'm your nanny."

"You and I both know that's temporary. It was never meant to be permanent. On either side."

"So you're just going to tell Jared I'm replacing him? You aren't going to confront him over the checks? Report this to the police? To the insurance company?"

"I think if we can correct the situation now we'll move forward. No one has to be the wiser."

I shake my head. "No one but the next company he works for. Then when he starts pilfering from their till how are you going to feel?"

"I'm going to feel like I did what I needed to do to correct my situation."

The bigger picture is coming into play. Protector mode. It's all about himself and his stuff. "I never saw you as selfish like this. He could really damage another company. And they might not have endless resources like the Treyhunes to be able to recover."

It doesn't seem right, arguing here in the park. Parks are happy places. Fun places where kids and families interact and play.

Not disagreeing about whether to send your best friend to jail.

"The Treyhunes might be able to recover financially, but you have no idea how this is affecting me emotionally. I need to do what I need to do. What I think is right."

Those lips that kiss me with such abandonment and fire now admonish me for trying to convince him to do the right thing.

I'm not sure I'll ever see those lips the same way again.

.

MESMERIZED

THE NEXT COUPLE of days go by without conversing with Court except for the polite hellos and goodbyes. His job offer lingers like a storm cloud between us.

A storm cloud named Justice.

The girls are asleep and I'm in Court's office making a step-by-step list to start the process of finding someone to homeschool Team Twin, but I find it hard to concentrate on that task.

I understand Court's hesitancy about bringing Jared's bad deeds to light, but to think that he might go out in the world and do this all over again doesn't sit well with me.

Neither does Court's attitude of as long as it isn't him, he's not going to worry about it.

Court believes Jared wouldn't do this to anyone else. That he probably felt like he was borrowing the money, and had visions of replacing it before anyone found out.

The bottom line is that it's Court's money and he can choose to ignore this if he wants to.

His interest now is what Jared needed the money for. He's afraid his friend is in some kind of trouble.

Court is more heroic than I ever would be.

"Are you still mad at me?"

I don't look up, as I know my expression will answer his question. My nonresponse will probably answer it as well.

"There are things you don't understand."

His voice cuts deep, opening a part of my heart to hear what he has to say. "Then help me understand, because I'm having a hard time."

He sits next to me on the loveseat. His shirt is wrinkled, his eyes tired-looking. This situation is taking its toll on Court.

"When we were kids, Jared always had one foot in juvey. My family and I tried to steer him away from his craziness, but he always went back. Something always drew him to the other side of the law. I lost count of how many times I rescued him out of one situation after another."

"Why and how did you remain friends? Didn't you get tired of his ways?"

"At times. But Jared was the only real friend I had. He didn't want me as his friend for what I could do for him. He couldn't care less. At least that's how I perceived it back then."

"That contrasts what we uncovered with the checks. He took from you."

"And as weird as this sounds, it's not his character. That's why I'm having a hard time with it. If he did take the money I'm sure his intent is to pay it back."

"But how much more damage would he cause before he paid it back? That's a lot of money, Court. A lot. Most people couldn't reimburse that amount unless they win the lottery or something."

"If I could find out why he needed the money I know everything would fall into place. Motivation, reason."

He hasn't mentioned me taking over the job since that day in the park. But we haven't talked much either since that day, so it still might be in his mind. "If I take the position from him, he wouldn't have the chance to pay you back."

"I never said he would pay it back. I said he would have visions of paying it back."

We could go around this rose bush forever. "So, what's the plan? Do you even have a plan?"

"I do."

"I'm listening."

"We are leaving in a week for Daytona. Jared will go with us. He always loved the track. While we're there, I'm going to offer him a job with the team. A job that doesn't have anything to do with finances. I'll work him into the R&D, research and development part of the team. He is good with numbers, and we could use his expertise in that field."

I shake my head. "You are a better man than I am. This is crazy, you know."

"I look out for my friends. Loyalty means a lot to me."

"Even when they aren't loyal to you."

"Jared is loyal. He's misguided at times, but he's loyal."

At least I know one thing. If I did take the job, I probably never would be fired.

WE ARRIVE IN Daytona hot, tired and ready to be out of the car. Team Twin doesn't travel well unless they're in an airplane, I guess.

Jared follows us, and he's bringing a guest.

A woman.

That woman he met at church.

Her name is Stace and she appears quite taken with Jared. I wonder how taken she'll be when she finds out he's going to be a traveling kind of guy.

I admit I was surprised when Court told me she was coming, and I was even more surprised when he said I'd be sharing the motor home with her. So, me, Stace and Team Twin will stay in Treyhune motor home number one, and Court and Jared will be in Treyhune motor home number two.

I have no idea how many motor homes there are.

I also want to warn her away from Jared, and I told Court as much when he told me about her joining us.

"Let nature run its course. Jared doesn't commit. If you want to warn her about anything, let it be that. But she'll figure it out soon enough."

We aren't at the track ten minutes, and we are draped with enough credentials to weigh down a two-hundred-pound man. I immediately locate a couple of safety pins and pin Team Twin's credentials to their shirts, knowing otherwise they will lose them.

Not that they need credentials. Everybody knows them and loves them.

I have purposely not called my parents these last few days. The less they know the better. And since they don't have all these credentials, I'm not worried about running into them. Trust me, I'm not leaving the immediate area.

The girls and I hang back as reporters talk to Court. Jared and Stace stay in the spotlight. To say I'm having a hard time being around Jared is an understatement.

I see him in a new light now. And it's not a flattering one.

Court is still cordial with him and even laughs with him. How does he do that?

I just want to blurt out "I know what you've done and I'm not as forgiving as your friend." Looking Jared in the eye is impossible now. I'm afraid I'll reveal my anger at the situation.

Having not conversed with Stace much yet, I'm not sure how I'll act toward her.

The motor home is complete luxury reminding me of the plane. Soft leather seats, fancy fixtures, granite counter tops. Bristol and Darling come in with me, and we bring in our suitcases.

We unpack our bags in the air-conditioned motor home.

"I want to stay in here," Bristol says. "It feels good. It's not so hot."

"You might not be as hot outside if you let me do something with that hair." The words come out before I can stop them.

But I don't regret them.

"I don't want you to do anything with my hair."

"Me either," Darling adds as they join forces together on the plush couch.

"I haven't touched your hair, and I'm not going to now. But don't you think your cousins' hair looks nice?"

"We're not them," Darling says, a pout clearly on her face.

"Yeah, we're us." Bristol crosses her arms in a defiant move.

A blast of heat comes in as the door opens. Stace walks in, dragging a suitcase behind her.

"Hi." She looks like the heat hasn't bothered her at all.

"Hi. It's tight quarters in here, but there's room in the back for you to put your bag."

I sit at the table so she can pass by without running into me. She returns immediately and joins Bristol and Darling on the couch. "Do you mind if I sit here?" she asks as she sits.

"No." Team Twin stares her down, but it doesn't seem to bother her.

"You girls are pretty. I love your hair."

"Ha," Bristol sits up for a moment and sticks her tongue out at me.

"Told you so."

"Wow," Stace says. "That's not nice."

"It's a lost battle. Their hair, not the tongue. That I can tame."

"Shelby's always on us about our hair." Bristol flops against the back of the couch.

"She should be," Stace says. "It's a mess."

Now the twins not only have a confused look about them, but I'm sure I do too.

"You just said you liked our hair," Bristol challenges.

"I do like it," Stace says. "I like the color. I like that it's long, and I'm sure it's pretty when it's brushed out."

"Nobody knows what it looks like when it's brushed out." I feel a kinship with this girl who has the same heart I do about the girls' hair.

"Maybe we'll play beauty shop later." Stace is very matter-of-fact in her tone. Like it's going to happen.

Team Twin slinks further away from Stace to the total opposite end of the couch. "Are you a beauty shop person?" Darling asks.

"No. I own a nail salon."

"Oh." They perk up at this knowledge. So do I. A business owner. Just who Jared needs to latch onto. Somebody else whose money he can take.

I smile like I haven't had those thoughts, wishing I could adopt Court's attitude about the situation.

Court didn't tell me when the big showdown was going to happen with Jared, but I can't imagine Court waiting until Saturday, race day.

"Do you like to travel?" I ask Stace. Maybe I can get a feel if she'll stick around after the big promotion. Demotion. Promotion. Whatever it is.

"I love to travel. My half sister lives in Peru, and I go there as often as I can. I've also taken my mother on a couple of trips in the past year."

That's going to be good news for Jared. Maybe he can make traveling around to tracks sound as exciting as Peru. Although, maybe he'll have a home base and not have to travel around so much.

I'll have to ask Court.

"Are you two okay?" Stace asks Team Twin.

"They're fine," I answer. "They're just making sure you're not going to whip out a brush."

Stace waves her palm in the air. "No chance. You wouldn't catch me tackling that mess. Not in a million years."

She proceeds to search through her purse, and I'm reminded again how pretty she is. She's all matching, too, with her pretty blue sundress, color-coordinated sandals and handbag. Her nails even compliment her outfit.

I wonder if she gives how-to-coordinate lessons.

Not that I have the items to coordinate. I'd have to do a lot of shopping first. Which I have no time, money or inclination to do.

The door to the RV opens. Court and Jared come in. Stace immediately looks up from her search mission and ditches her purse. Her eyes light up as she sees Jared and my heart lurches.

Not fair.

She looks as mesmerized by him as I am by Court.

I have to figure out how to subtly warn her away from Jared.

Even though I don't know her, I'm sure she deserves better than a good-looking embezzler.

Anyone would.

MODESTY

THE GUYS BRING an air of excitement with them. The atmosphere at the track is one like I've never experienced. You can't help but be taken in by all the activity and people.

Court's gaze catches mine, but he keeps his distance. "I'm sure you ladies are hungry. I wanted to let you know we are having food delivered in. It will be here within the hour."

"Good, I'm hungry," Bristol says.

"Jared and I are headed to the garage," Court says.

"Team meeting," Jared jokes.

Court's expression isn't saying joke, and I wonder if he's going to talk to Jared now. Tonight.

Maybe so. Maybe he wants the talk out of the way, so it won't be a distraction to the real reason he's here.

They leave and when the food arrives a short time later, I find myself not very hungry. I'm worried about how it's going with Court and Jared.

The girls are shoving down the food like they've never eaten before, while Stace doesn't eat much at all.

I also received a text from my mom saying they've arrived at the track. I text back a smiley face and leave it at that.

Good thing her phone doesn't tell her that she's probably less than a mile from me.

The urge to see my parents is strong, but not strong enough to deal with that whole situation here. We already have too much drama going on.

Not that Court and I are anything but a few kisses. Oh, and if he has his way, his next CFO. That's one job offer I won't be accepting.

But why complicate matters now?

As we are cleaning up the leftovers, the door opens and Jared walks in. I can tell right away everything has changed. Disappointment is written all over his face, and I try to control my tongue.

"Stace," he says in a calm tone, "we're heading out. We'll leave as soon as you gather your things and get to the car."

"What? We just arrived?"

He smiles and I know in that instant she'll go along with whatever he says. Some men have that power, and Jared James is one of them. "I'll explain in the car."

"You're leaving, Uncle Jared?" Bristol asks.

"I am. Come give Uncle Jared a bye hug."

Team Twin jumps up as Stace heads to the back of the RV. Good thing she didn't unpack anything.

The twins squeal with laughter as Jared hugs them bye and tickles them at the same time. Right now, I'm so conflicted. How can this man be so good, yet so bad?

Stace walks back to the front area of the RV and Jared takes her bag.

"Bye, everyone," she says as she walks down the steps out of the RV.

"Bye," I say.

Team Twin remains silent. Probably still mad about her comments regarding their hair.

Jared holds the door open with his free hand and starts walking down the steps. Before he takes the last one, he turns and looks at me. "I hope you enjoy the job, Shelby."

No sarcasm, no anger.

No emotion at all which is scarier than the other scenarios.

"What job?" Bristol asks as the door shuts. "Aren't you going to be our nanny anymore?"

I have no answer for these children as I have no idea what Court has told Jared.

AS DARKNESS FALLS, so does a soft rain. A dreaded complication during race weekend. Team Twin has fallen asleep on the couch, and I've settled in one of the easy chairs waiting on Court.

He still hasn't returned.

But I'm ready for him when he does.

A part of me wants to quit this whole gig, text my parents, and stay with them for a couple of days.

This is a crazy world of friends betraying friends, friends not facing facts and guilty people making the innocent feel guilty.

And I thought there was drama in the Dale situation.

That pales in comparison to what has taken place in the Treyhune household over the last few days.

And in the Treyhune RV as well.

My heart not only aches for Court, but it aches for Jared in a weird way. It aches for the fact that he felt like he had a right to do what he did. It's the only way to explain how he acted when he showed up here hours ago. Honestly, he looked like the victim.

Not the criminal.

I wonder if he took the job Court offered. Or maybe he just said see you later and left.

Everything.

All those years of friendship.

He should have thought of that before writing checks to himself.

I'm almost lulled to sleep by the tapping of the rain on the RV, so when Court enters, it's anticlimactic from how I envisioned it.

I pictured him bursting in the door going on and on about Jared's refusal of his job offer, or whatever it was that went down between the two of them.

When I fully open my eyes, it's to see him, his hair slightly dampened by the rain, settling into the chair across from mine.

"How're things?" he asks, running his hand through his hair.

"Things are things." I'm not sure what he expects me to say.

"Everybody asleep?" he asks, staring at the couch.

"They are," I say feeling strange answering the obvious.

"Is Stace back in one of the bedrooms?"

His attention now focused on me, I look at him. "Stace left. With Jared. Hours ago."

His eyes widen and his expression turns a little crazed. "They left? Why didn't you call me?"

"I thought you knew."

"How would I know?"

"How would I know you didn't know? And did you tell him I was taking his job?"

One of the twins starts to stir and he motions me to the back of the RV. We end up in the bedroom at the back, sitting on the bed.

"Tell me what happened." Court takes my hands in his as he speaks.

I want to jerk them out because I'm not sure what went down, but I find the feel of his touch comforting. I explain to him what happened when Jared came to the RV earlier.

"I didn't tell him you would be taking the job. He assumed I was taking the job from him and giving it to you."

"Why would he assume that? I've never told him my background. As far as he knows, I'm just a nanny."

"He told me he Googled you when he was interested in going out with you and found out you used to work as a CFO for an engineering company. He always wondered why you took a job as a nanny."

"Oh. Well, that's a lot of assuming, isn't it? Did you let him go? Transfer him? Ask him about the checks at all?"

"I told him I thought the track was the place for him. That I needed a guy in the shop working with the crew chiefs. It's kind of embarrassing what went down next."

"I promise I won't laugh at your embarrassment."

"He said he knew I was falling for you and would do anything to keep you here in Florida. Even ditch my best friend."

"Are you serious? He said that?"

"He did. And I tried to convince him he was wrong, but I didn't do a very good job of it."

"Let me get this straight. He steals from you, and you offer him a job with less access to the cash, and he accuses you of being in love with your nanny. I don't follow the train of thought at all."

"I couldn't convince him I'm not in love with you because I am."

If I thought my burden was heavy a little while ago, I was wrong. How can he be in love with me? "I don't think you are in love with me. I think you are curious about me, or taken with the fact that Team Twin likes me. But I don't think you're in love with me."

"You're the first person who's made me feel anything since before MaryLeigh died."

"And that's what you're in love with. That fact."

"No. I'm in love with Shelby. The woman who I catch gazing at me when she thinks I'm not looking. The woman whose laugh I can't wait to hear, so I ditch my job and come home early. The woman who let's my kids be who they are out of a respect for me and my crazy ways that need to be changed. That's who I'm in love with."

"Court—"

"Say it, Shelby. Say you love me."

I don't understand this. I don't understand him. I don't understand how a heart can melt this fast with an understanding that even if it doesn't understand much, it can't refute truth. "I love you."

The words are out, in the air for him to hear. For him to process. For him to embrace.

His lips cover mine and we fall onto the bed like it's the most natural thing ever. Within seconds we are side by side, kissing, touching. I run my hands down his arms as his hands delicately caress the hair around my face. He leans up on one elbow, his gaze never leaving me.

"This thing with Jared," he starts, "will be easier to handle with you by my side."

"He already thinks I'm by your side if you know what I mean. He thinks I stole his job."

"When we get back we're going to confront him about the checks. I know that's the right thing to do. We'll lay it all out and see what he has to say."

"As much as I want justice to prevail, I find it hard to focus on that while lying in a bed with you. I'd rather be kissing you."

He leans over, capturing my lips in his. His tongue gently traces my lips, and I find myself not being able to kiss him deeply enough. Like I'm thirsting and he's the fountain.

He sits up and grabs the bottom of my shirt. My mind travels back years to that first night with Paul.

But this is different.

Very different, I reason as Court starts to push my shirt up.

He said he loved me.

So did Paul.

"No."

He quickly lets go. "I'm sorry. I thought…"

I place my finger on his lips. "I thought I was ready for this, but I'm not."

"It's okay," he says. He runs his hand through his hair. "I don't know what I'm thinking. The girls are out there. All this with Jared. I'm not thinking straight, obviously."

I'm not sure from where this sense of modesty has come, I just know it's undeniable. "I'm to blame, too. I shouldn't have let it go this far. We've just said the words 'I love you.' Can we explore what those words really mean in our lives before we cross lines that can never be uncrossed?"

"There will never be any going back with us, Shelby. Only going forward. But I'm willing to wait however long it takes for that to happen."

The space is cramped, but he scoots off the bed with ease. He leans over, kissing me thoroughly. "I do love you, Shelby," he says as he exits the room.

My face heats thinking about the route we were headed.

The route that I've taken before with men that has led to only one thing.

Disaster.

Nothing ever lasting, obviously.

No, if that's going to happen with Court, I'm making sure he's going to be forever.

And right now, even though we've spoken those three words, I'm not convinced forever is in our future.

There's still too much he doesn't know about me.

MEET

THE RAIN FROM THE previous night has led to sunny, blue skies this morning. I pour coffee as I watch Team Twin continue to sleep, that hair sprawled across the soft, white leather couch.

When I came out of the bedroom last night, Court was gone. I figured he would be. Instead of awaking with shame, like I could have, I woke this morning renewed.

Renewed with faith that Court and I will last forever.

I know how I feel when I think about him, and the feeling is one of completeness. Like he makes me feel whole, secure in who we are together, because for the first time, who we are together is way more important than who I am apart from him.

I can honestly say that is a first.

And I can honestly say I've been thinking about my faith. That service last Sunday spoke to my heart, then Court's confession of love last night fueled the notion that we aren't alone in this world.

Who but God could have orchestrated my life in this manner? Here I am, in love with a man that is the exact type of man I vowed to stay away from. Court has captured my heart, and I think it's because God captured it first.

For the first time I'm excited for a man to meet my parents. Of course, Court doesn't know he's going to meet them, and there's a conversation Court and I need to have first, but I'm filled with a calm, peaceful, yet excited feeling that doesn't make sense.

When Court shows up twenty minutes later, he bursts through the door with a vase of beautiful red roses and a box of donuts.

He kisses me quickly, something I'm sure he takes advantage of because the girls are still asleep. "Presents for my girls. Flowers for you, donuts for Team Twin."

I like how he uses the name I made up for them. "Are we allowed to share?" I ask, surprised at how glad I am that he's here. I haven't experienced this feeling before. And I'm thrilled with it.

"Of course you can." He sets the donuts and the flowers on the counter. "I think I'm going to wake them up. We need to get going. Besides, I don't trust myself around the woman I'm in love with. She might corrupt me."

"Ha." I push him away from me. "It's the other way around. But before you wake them up, I have something I need to talk to you about."

"Uh, oh." He slides into the breakfast booth. "This sounds serious."

I slide in across from him. "It's serious, but not in the way you are thinking. It's more of a serious step."

He reaches across the table and holds my hand. "I'm curious."

"My parents are here at the race track—"

"Your parents? Why didn't you say so earlier? Where are they?"

I swallow, knowing an explanation, a long one is forthcoming. "I'm not sure where they are staying. I haven't told them I'm here."

His expression says perplexed. "Why not?"

"It's a complicated hot mess, but the bottom line is my family are just plain people. My dad is the biggest race fan around, and your dad is the hero of all heroes in their house."

"That's cool. My dad has a lot of fans."

"Until last night I didn't want to introduce you to them."

"Why not?"

Here it is. Time to lay it all out. Might as well find out now if he's the one. I can't explain how bold I feel as I'm about to reveal my past. I want to tell this man all about who I am.

Who I really am. Not who he thinks I am. He needs to know, and I need to know now if it will change things.

I take a deep breath, and I'm calmer than I ever thought I'd be at this stage of a relationship with someone like Court. "Because. We are so different, Court. You and me. My family, your family. I grew up in a trailer park, kids made fun of me in school, we never went without but we never had a lot."

He stares at me like he's waiting for me to go on. When I don't he half smiles. "Is that all you've got? Where you grew up doesn't change how I feel about you. And if we go to one of your class reunions, I'll call out the kids who made fun of you. How's that."

Closing my eyes momentarily, I shake my head. When I look at Court again, I see the love in his eyes. I pray he's telling the truth. "Court. I've been trying my whole life to be something. Anything. The story I told that day to Team Twin? It was a true story. That little girl was me."

"Shelby, I love that the little girl was you. How you grew up has made you an amazing woman. You have so much compassion. So much love."

I straighten my shoulders. "What if I told you I don't really even like wine?"

He kisses the back of my hand. "I'd say you were an awfully good pretender."

My heart jolts, my eyes tear. "That's what I'm trying to tell you. I've been pretending my whole life. My whole life." I wiggle my hand out of his and start to stand.

"Then it's time to stop." His voice is as loud as it can be in the RV with the girls still asleep on the couch. "My heart knows the real Shelby Madison, the woman I've fallen in love with. Now I think it's time to meet your parents."

I love this moment. I love how I believe in Courts words. They've grounded me, not made me wary or worried. "You have no idea what you are saying. My dad is going to have a fan moment. That is after he yells at me for not telling him who I've been working for."

"They don't know you've been working for me?"

I laugh. "No. Are you kidding? They would have been on your front door faster than you can say race fan. And, this is my dad's first race. My mom scrimped and saved to bring him here. Court, this will make his life."

"I love how excited you are talking about it. I can tell they mean a lot to you."

"They do. Something else I didn't know until last night. But your 'I love you' changed everything."

"What're your mom and dad's names? I'll call right now and get two passes to our suite. They will enjoy the view."

"Herman and Penny Madison. And my dad will enjoy the view if he doesn't pass out from the excitement."

"He'll be fine. Call them. I'll call who I need to, then you can walk over to the gate to meet them. The girls and I will wait here."

After a brief conversation that totally confuses my parents, I walk to the gate that I entered through yesterday.

Yesterday.

It feels like a lifetime ago.

Jared and Stace are gone. I have no idea where Court and Jared's friendship is going at this point.

Court said he loved me.

And now he's meeting my parents.

I feel good about this meeting. No trepidation like when I introduced them to Dale. No, I feel like this is going to be a whole new experience.

Some guy with a Treyhune Motorsports shirt had brought me the passes, so when I spot Mom and Dad and wave, the passes are visible. Now Dad really looks confused. They produce all the proper documentation that allows them through the gate and into my arms for a hug.

"Shelby Ray Madison. What have you gone and done? I hope you didn't spend a lot of money for these passes. We don't want you spending your hard-earned money on us."

I hug my mom while answering my dad. "I haven't spent a dime. But we do need to have a quick talk."

"Okay," my dad says. "Talk."

"Well, you know I've been working in Florida. And you know I'm a nanny. What you don't know is who I'm a nanny for. I know you know the name. Court Treyhune."

My dad's expression is priceless and I want to take a picture, but I don't think it would be a good idea. I can't imagine the look on his face if I were to tell him Court loves me.

I'm not going there. One heart attack moment at a time. That one can wait.

Besides, I don't want to share that with anyone yet. I want to keep those words all to myself, close to my heart for as long as I can.

"You are babysitting Court Treyhune's children?"

I laugh at the disbelief in my dad's tone. And at the how he makes the situation real by using the word babysitting. "I'm their nanny. Twin girls—"

"Bristol and Darling," my dad interrupts.

I momentarily forgot my dad knows all things Treyhune. "Yes, that's right. So now, if you follow me, we are going to the RV. Court and his girls are there waiting for us."

"We're going to *meet* Court Treyhune?"

"You are. And he's excited to meet you." I say the words with confidence. I know they are true. Mama's wary expression and lack of words doesn't escape my notice.

We walk the short distance to the RV with me having to nudge my dad along every now and then. Apparently he's star struck every other step. I don't know who is who, so star struck I'm not.

"Shelby, this is amazing. Did you see that? Hank Favor just walked by. I could have reached out and touched him. Hank Favor!"

I don't know Hank except through my dad. If my relationship with Court goes like my heart says it's going, my dad will have the opportunity to see and possibly meet any race personality that he wants.

Maybe they'll all come to our wedding.

Wedding?

Shivers run up my arm at the direction my thoughts just went. I don't want to move too far ahead, but being in love is a good first step to eventually getting married.

We arrive at the RV. I stop outside the door. "Dad. Are you okay?"

His eyes look glazed over like he's had a few drinks. But I know he's high on this atmosphere. He's loved and admired this world for all these years, and now he's actually living in the middle of it.

And he's about to meet his favorite driver's son.

Who loves his daughter.

I let that thought settle on me before I open the door.

"I'm good," Dad says.

"All right. Let's go in." I open the door, the cool air hitting me along with the scent of the flowers Court brought me this morning.

It's also very quiet. Very quiet for Team Twin being awake and hyped-up on sugar if they've eaten those donuts. The scent of the flowers turns sickly sweet, turning my stomach.

Did they leave?

Is there a note telling me they're gone?

It's not like there's many places to hide here in this RV.

My mom steps into the RV right behind me. My dad is almost all the way up the stairs when Team Twin run out from one of the rooms in the back. "Shelby!"

They run to me and hug me. "We wanted to surprise you. We saved you a donut. Dad told us we didn't have to, that you would understand if we ate them all, but we wanted you to have one. It's right here."

They point to a plate that is sitting on the counter. The plate is covered with a paper towel.

"Thank you. I appreciate that. You know how much I love donuts. Girls, these are my parents. Mr. and Mrs. Madison."

"Hi, Mr. and Mrs. Madison," Team Twin says.

"Hello, girls." Mama speaks while my dad nods. I think he's still in shock.

"Hello, Mr. and Mrs. Madison."

I swear I have to keep my dad from falling backward when Court speaks.

"It's nice to meet you," Court continues, offering his hand. "Your daughter has been amazing with my girls. We're lucky to have her, aren't we?"

He looks at Bristol and Darling who nod.

Mama shakes his hand. "Very nice to meet you. I'm glad Shelby has fit into your lives so well. She is a sweet girl."

When my dad shakes Court's hand, Court places his other hand over the handshake. "Great to meet you, Mr. Madison. Shelby has spoken highly of you."

Yes, those are tears in my dad's eyes.

Honestly. I wouldn't lie about a thing like this.

"It's an honor to meet you. An honor."

Wow. My dad's voice holds emotion I haven't heard since my college graduation ceremony when he told me how proud he was of me.

There's a warmth in this RV that stems from our hearts.

I take note that after all the introductions, when all has settled, I'm standing right next to Court.

Where I know I should be standing.

SUNDAY AFTERNOON, back in Hampton Cove, I unpack my

suitcase, my eyes tearing up every time I think of my dad and the weekend he experienced. He couldn't say thank you enough, and I finally had to tell him he didn't need to say it again. That Court and I both knew he was thankful.

Everybody we met was nice and cordial. And we met a lot of people. I will never keep the names straight. Court stayed with us as much as possible, but most of the weekend was spent with my parents and Team Twin.

Team Twin no longer call my mama and dad Mr. and Mrs. Madison. Nope, now they are Ms. Maddy and Mr. Herms. My dad blushed at the shortening of his name by the girls.

But now we're back to reality. Back to trying to figure out the Jared situation. I know it was good for Court to have something else to occupy his mind for a couple of days. Betrayal runs deep and when it's your best friend, it's especially hard to take.

I've already arranged for Bristol and Darling to go next door tomorrow to hang out with Phoebe while Court and I go to his office and talk to Jared.

Long after the girls are in bed and the clock tells us it's now another day, Court and I sit at the edge of the pool, our feet dangling in the warm water, preparing for the morning and the revelation it will bring.

We've spent hours talking the situation to death, and there's not much more that can be said until we hear Jared's explanation.

But I don't feel tired or like going in right now. The night beckons us to linger.

"It means a lot to me that you accepted my parents the way you did. We all felt at home and welcomed by everyone. And my dad, I think he's at home probably ready to faint by now. Can you say fan overload?"

He laughs. "Your parents were great. They were gracious and nice to everyone. They seemed to fit right in."

Fit right in. Words I'd never thought I'd hear from someone like Court Treyhune regarding me and my family. I never fit in Paul's world or Dale's world, but Court has embraced me knowing full well who I am and where I come from.

This love with Court is different from the other times I thought I was in love. I'm not anxious about things. Worried about our families meshing or not. No, I'm relaxed and calm when it comes to Court.

Until he kisses me.

That's the only aspect regarding him that makes my heart go wild.

And that's the way it should be.

MORNING

COURT'S OFFICE is cold.

Not cool, cold.

I'm glad I brought my sweater.

The atmosphere is tense waiting for Jared to arrive. Susan knows we are expecting him.

I love how Court approached her when we walked in a short while ago. He picked up his mail from her desk, then said, "Shelby and I will be in my office. We're expecting Jared, so send him in when he gets here."

We're.

Love this.

Don't love the situation, but I love that we are handling it together. Together we'll push through. I know Court has way more at stake here than I do, but there's no bigger stake than Court's heart, which I have a stake in.

So, what's important to Court is important to me.

Even though I'm prepared to see Jared, I still jump when the door clicks open and he walks in. His eye's narrow when he sees me, indicating he didn't expect me to be here.

He thinks I'm the enemy after his job.

Nothing could be further from the truth.

If I thought the office was cold when we walked in, it's now about to form icicles if it were possible.

Jared looks at Court. "I didn't know Shelby would be here. Do you need to rub it in more? Choosing your girl over your best friend?"

Court sits in his chair and motions for Jared to sit in one of the two chairs across the desk. As Jared sits, I do too, and I notice he scoots his chair away from me.

I'm confused by his blatant disregard for his friend and the situation. He has written checks and deposited them in his account, yet he's acting like Court and I are the enemy. Of course, he doesn't know that we know.

Courts taps his fingers on the stack of copies we printed from the bank.

The evidence.

"Jared, this is a hard conversation to have with you. But it's one that must be had. I don't know where to begin, so I'll let you look at these papers, then we can talk."

Jared's guard is fully on as he picks up the papers Court has slid across the desk. I watch Jared carefully as he looks at them. Body language and facial expressions can reveal so much.

And my stomach knots at what Jared is revealing.

Shock, surprise and confusion.

His expression clearly shouts he knows nothing about these checks.

Nothing.

"I've seen this vendor pop up recently in the books and I've been meaning to ask you about them. I was puzzled as to what type of media we were adding and why." Jared's voice holds an honesty that can't be denied.

Court leans forward in his chair, and I watch the two of them, like a drama unfolding.

"You see we've printed the check copies from the bank. You see we know you put those checks into your bank account. I'm disappointed."

"Jared didn't put those checks in his account."

Both men turn to me as I speak. Both men have equally surprised looks on their faces.

"He's been framed."

It's written all over Jared's face.

"Framed?" Court asks.

"You believe I've been framed?" Jared asks, swallowing hard like he's just accepting that fact.

I stand. "I could tell the minute you looked at those checks you didn't have a clue as to why you were sitting here. Somebody forges your signature very well, though."

"Janice."

Jared speaks that one word and it's like we all sigh the last puzzle piece into place, revealing the bigger picture. But there are still many unanswered questions.

Court's eyes glisten, reminding me of my father's that day in the RV. Jared's demeanor is no longer as guarded and the icicles have melted into a heap of water we're all trying to wade through.

"Why would Janice put the money in your account? With all the money issues you've had lately, the money can't still be there." Court has stood now and is pacing his office.

"There's something you need to know, Court." Jared shoves his hands in his pockets, his GQ look rumpling and wrinkling fast.

"What?"

"Janice is MaryLeigh's daughter."

I watch everything about Court shatter until his hands grip the desk for support. "Daughter? Impossible."

"I wish it were. I wish I had told you sooner."

"Jared. She can't be. It's physically impossible. How old is Janice?"

"Eighteen. MaryLeigh had her when she was sixteen."

Court, still steadying himself with the help of the desk, rolls his eyes momentarily, like he's doing the math.

Pain, anguish, confusion is written all over Court's face. He shakes his head like doing so will shake these insinuations into place. "Who exactly was MaryLeigh Rigby, Jared? Because I don't think I knew my wife at all."

Court's gaze steels as the icicles threaten to form again. "But apparently you did."

THE SUBJECT OF the forged checks falls to the back burner as Jared tells Court about Janice. How MaryLeigh had gotten pregnant by a local boy, refused to tell the boy about the baby, claiming it was somebody else's.

"She knew if she owned up to that baby being Joe Campbell's he would have insisted on marrying her. The last thing MaryLeigh wanted was to live in Jocelyn, North Carolina, the rest of her life."

"And this Joe believed her? About the baby not being his?"

"He didn't at first. Was pretty insistent, but lucky for MaryLeigh there had been a hoity-toity city guy that had been in town for a while, and she did cozy up to him. He didn't take to her in the way she wanted, which was a way to hightail it out of town, but nobody knew that. The right words and right memories were convincing enough for Joe to back off and leave

MaryLeigh alone. MaryLeigh pretended she found Jesus, gave the baby up for adoption, then proceeded to make a totally new image for herself."

"And you never thought any of this was important to tell me."

"Come on, Court. I was under her spell same as you. And of course I wanted to tell you, but she swore me to secrecy. Besides, I didn't think you'd end up marrying her. Man, you two started dating and bam, before anybody knew what was happening, you two were hitched."

"Yeah, she was quick to get me to the altar."

"After that, it seemed it was all water under the bridge so to speak. You guys were happy. I'd never seen her so happy."

"She was happy, all right. I'd never seen a person change so much in such a short time. All these things I thought I knew about her, I didn't know at all. But I adjusted."

Never have I been so glad to have come clean with somebody in my life. I can't imagine keeping my past from Court now. After all he's been through regarding MaryLeigh and with the revelation he received today. My slate with Court is clean. I have nothing to hide from this man.

"She was happy, Court," Jared says. "And when Janice came to me and told me her story, I couldn't turn her down. I thought I'd help her out for a little while with a job, then when she was on her feet she could get a better job and she'd be gone."

"I don't even remember what she looks like."

"She favors MaryLeigh, but not like Bristol and Darling. But still, when I knew you were coming around, I'd send her off on an errand. I didn't want you to make the connection."

"Well, I didn't. And now look at this mess. She even switched the letters of your name around to make up this fake company. I still don't understand where the money went if she put it in your account. Not only did you not notice it was there, it's not there anymore."

"That's not as surprising to me as it is to you. Apparently Janice is a lot like MaryLeigh in that I was sucked into Janice's web. She was doing great at the job, so when I complained about paying bills and such on a personal level, she offered to do that for me as well. I gave her online access to my bank account so she could pay my bills."

"Wow" is all I can say.

"Yeah. As much as I like handling monies on a corporate level, managing my own bank account seemed insignificant and nothing but trouble. I was more than eager to hand it over to Janice when she offered." Jared shrugs his shoulders then nods toward Court's computer. "Do you mind? I can look at my account now. We'll have some answers."

An hour and a half later we had all the answers. Janice had deposited the money into Jared's account then the next day sent it out to creditors. One transaction paid in full for a nice double-wide trailer.

JANICE HAD ESSENTIALLY embezzled a house.

Incredible!

She had also pilfered some of Jared's money, starting with small amounts, but as the months went along, the amounts got bigger.

"What do we do now?" Court asks after we are sitting down, amazed at all Janice has done. "No matter the circumstances, I can't prosecute MaryLeigh's daughter. I just can't."

"Then you can't turn it over to your insurance company to recoup the money," I offer. "They'll want their money back and prosecute her."

"Then it's settled," Court says. "We'll take this as a loss. A huge loss. We'll let her go, of course, but Jared, get with her. See what she needs. I don't ever want her to want for anything."

"Do you want me to tell her you know about her? Who she is?"

Court doesn't answer immediately. If I could see inside his mind, I bet I'd see dozens of wheels going in different directions. I'm still in shock at all that has been discovered this morning. I can't imagine how Court is truly feeling.

"No. Not right now. She has enough going on and she's obviously overwhelmed. Tell her you discovered the checks. Hire the best therapist available and tell Janice that if she goes for help, the company won't prosecute her. Tell her to keep in touch. I take it the baby's father isn't in the picture."

"Nope. Long gone. Doesn't even know about the baby. At least that's what she says."

"Okay. She might need some help then. Make sure you don't lose sight of her."

Jared stands and leans against the wall. "I never would have let her hurt you, Court. You or the girls. You have to know that."

Court looks at his friend. "I do know that."

"Yet you somehow thought I would embezzle money from you. I have to be honest. That hurts. Right here." Jared balls his hand into a fist and taps his heart.

"I'm sorry."

Jared walks over to the desk and picks up the check copies. "You let these pieces of paper override years of friendship and trust."

Court locks his hand behind his head. "You're right. I let what I was seeing blur what I knew was the truth."

I wonder how much of a part I had in that. Was I quick to judge Jared? Were his smooth ways and good looks suspicious to me because of my recent past with Dale?

Cringing on the inside, I hope I didn't push Court to judge Jared unfairly. Of course, with my black and white mentality at times, once I saw that signature on those checks, I had only one verdict in mind.

"I went to your house that day, a few weeks back. I knew something was up when I saw the financials on your desk. And the copies of the checks. I thought you were showing Shelby everything because you wanted her to take over. But I was trying to give you the benefit of the doubt. What is it your mom always says, Court. What truth does your mom live by?"

Closing his eyes for a moment, Court shakes his head and opens his eyes. "You have to have faith. But you know I don't live by that."

Jared walks to the door and opens it. He looks at Court, then looks at me. Jared once again focuses on Court. "Maybe, for everybody's sake, you should."

He closes the door, leaving Court and me alone.

Alone with revelations from the past that have the power to change the future.

MISUNDERSTANDING

I PICK UP THE girls from Jenny and Stephen's right after lunch. It feels like I have worked a week already.

And it's only been a morning.

The girls are rambunctious once we return home and yet they reject my offer to swim.

"We don't want to swim." Bristol scrunches up her nose. "We want to do something else."

"Like what?" I ask.

Team Twin look at each other, and I notice a *look* passing between them. A look that means they know what's going on.

A part of me is scared at what they might come up with.

"We'll be right back."

I wait in the kitchen for them to return. When five minutes pass, and they don't, I start to become concerned. But before I can act on it, I hear them call my name.

"Shelby! Come back here."

Their tone doesn't sound frantic. It sounds excited.

Wondering what they could be up to, I walk into their room.

And stare.

Each one of them is holding a brush.

An actual hairbrush.

Chills race up my arms at the sight.

"We tried to brush our hair, but it's kind of hard. Can you help us?"

Fighting back tears, but not a smile, I walk to the girls. "Sure. Who's first?"

"Me," Bristol says, shoving her brush at me.

We all sit in the middle of their room. Bristol sits right in front of me, and I start at the bottom, slowly working my way up. Slowly being the operative word. I've said I'm sorry more than once at tugging her hair, and she's repeated it's okay just as many times.

Darling watches wide-eyed and curious.

"Mommy loved to brush our hair."

Bristol's words confuse me. "She did?"

"Yes. But we didn't like her to."

I continue to brush, not commenting. It's dangerous territory for sure.

"Maybe you can be our mommy now."

It's all I can do not to turn into a puddle on the floor. Keeping the pace of my brushing going, I hope I don't let on how her words have affected me. I know I love Court, and I know he loves me, but achieving a lifetime together takes more than those three words.

I run the brush from the top of her hair to the bottom and the full beauty of her dark black hair amazes me. It drapes to the floor and is as thick as molasses on a hot day.

"Beautiful," I whisper.

"It is?" Bristol asks.

"I want mine to look like that." Darling hands me her brush. "My turn."

Bristol's demeanor has changed as she sits and watches me brush out Darling's hair.

"Have you guys ever heard of Locks of Love?" I ask.

"What's that?" they ask.

"Someday, if you decide you ever want to cut your hair, you can donate what they cut off to an organization called Locks of Love. They make wigs for children who have cancer."

"Cancer?" Bristol asks. "That's what Mommy had. That's why she died. She had cancer."

"I know," I reply. "The kids that have to have chemotherapy need wigs so when their hair falls out they can still have hair if they want to."

"Oh," Darling says. "It's like when we put the toys in the box. We were helping kids who didn't have any toys. And our hair can help kids who don't have any hair."

"That's right." For some reason, Darling's hair is a little easier to brush. Maybe I have more skills having already brushed my way through Bristol's hair. Either way, it takes half the time. But her hair is just as beautiful. Since they did wash their hair last night, it's still clean.

"Girls. Let me take your picture."

They stand and I watch their hair fall elegantly past their waist. Their faces look lighter, like a weight has been lifted.

I take a picture with them smiling, then I have them turn around and take one from behind.

"Beautiful. Your daddy is going to be so surprised."

It's all I can do not to text the photo to Court, but I want to see his face when he sees his girls' beautiful hair.

"I know how we can really surprise daddy." Bristol has an I've-got-an-idea look on her face.

"How's that," I ask, sliding my phone back in my pocket.

"We can donate our hair to the kids with cancer. Like Mommy. Remember how happy Daddy was when we gave the kids our toys? He'll be happy that we want to help the kids with cancer."

Darling looks like Bristol has just announced the best idea ever in the world. "Yes. That's a great idea." Darling looks at me. "Can we? Can we surprise Daddy?"

"Please?" Bristol begs.

"Yes, please?" Darling begs even louder.

Court was pleased with the girls wanting to give away their toys to an organization that helped other kids. But this is a little different. This is their hair. "Girls, I know you want to surprise your dad, but we really should ask him first. This is a big step for you guys. Have you ever had short hair?"

"No. But Phoebe does and it looks really nice. We like it, don't we, Darling?"

"We do. Please let us surprise Daddy."

As much as I want to be a part of what I know would be a great surprise, I can't imagine taking them without asking Court. "Girls, this is a huge step. I'll text him and ask him if it's okay if you cut your hair. We won't say how much. He'll still be surprised, I promise."

The girls look disappointed, but I know it's the right thing to do. So I text him that the girls want to cut hair for kids with cancer.

I have to wait less than a minute for a response. "Sure. Sounds great."

I smile. "We've got the go-ahead. Are you girls ready?"

"Yes!"

After a quick call to Phoebe's mother, Teresa, to find out where their stylist is located, we drive over.

The girls become more nervous as their turn approaches. When the stylist, Robin, learns they want to give their hair to Locks of Love, she fawns all over Team Twin.

An hour later, with two bags of hair ready to mail off, we exit the salon. The girls' hair is cut in the same style, a bob just below their ears.

"We love our hair, Shelby. Thanks for taking us."

"It looks great, girls. I know your dad is going to like it, too."

I can't believe the difference in their appearance. Taylor and Saylor have nothing on these girls now.

We walk in the door and into the kitchen. Mrs. Stratton turns around and drops the bowl she's holding. It's a good thing it was plastic, but there are plenty of spaghetti noodles stuck to the floor.

"What has happened to their hair?" Mrs. Stratton can't take her eyes off the girls.

I bet she hasn't even noticed the noodles.

"Doesn't it look great? They wanted to surprise their dad."

"Surprise will be the understatement of the year. Decade."

"We had his permission. He just doesn't know what style they picked."

"We're gonna go look in the mirror." Team Twin runs down the hall, leaving me with a befuddled housekeeper. I grab a paper towel and start cleaning up the noodles.

Mrs. Stratton continues to stare at me. "I don't believe it. He gave you permission to take them to cut their hair?"

Grabbing another paper towel, I bend down and continue to do her job. "He did. Why does this surprise you so much? It was always a mess. Besides, they are donating the hair to Locks of Love. That's what's in the bags on the counter. We're going to print off the forms and send it tomorrow."

Mrs. Stratton finally regains some of her composure, and she sets the plastic colander she had dropped in the sink. "I'll have to boil more noodles," she mumbles, filling a pan with water. "This is the last thing I thought I'd ever see. That hair was their prized possession. Mr. Treyhune loved that hair. Again, I'm amazed at the transformation of that man. Thought I'd never see the day he let them cut their hair."

I toss the noodles I've scooped up into the trash then wash my hands. I dig my phone out of my purse and call up the text I sent to Court. "Here. See for yourself. He said it was fine."

Acting like she doesn't want to read it, but peering closer she squints, then squints again. "Says here the girls want to buy hair for kids with cancer. Where's the text about cutting the hair."

My heart starts beating extremely rapidly. I turn the phone around and scroll up. No. We are on the right text. I look at it. And look again.

Girls want to buy hair for kids with cancer.

Then his text, Sure. Sounds great.

Buy hair.

Cut hair.

Auto correct has possibly ruined my life.

I mean, I don't think Court will be that upset about the hair, regardless of what Mrs. Stratton thinks, but I think he should have been in on the decision making.

I tried.

Surely he will see this situation for what it is.

A misunderstanding.

After all, it is hair.

It will grow back.

And the kids are doing something great by donating their hair.

I slip my phone back in my purse not worried at all.

"HE'S HOME!"

Bristol's voice screams down the hall way. I haven't told them about the texting mix-up. They'll be thrilled it's going to be a surprise.

"Girls. Like we planned. Go in the living room and wait for me to say the word surprise. Hurry." I motion them toward the living room as I hear the garage door going back down.

It's almost eight o'clock. Mrs. Stratton tried to think of many reasons to stick around and "witness the carnage," as she put it, but finally she had to agree there was no good reason for her to stay.

Court had texted saying he was working late with Jared, making sure all the accounts had been updated with new passwords. They also looked for any more signs of money missing but hadn't found anything else.

He walks down the hall and looks around as he reaches me. I nod toward the living room indicating the girls are in there. I know he wants to kiss me, but doesn't.

Just like I want to kiss him and I refuse to entertain the thought that it might be my last kiss after he sees the girls hair.

"Why don't you have a seat right here?" I point to the bar stool. "Your girls have something they want to show you. It's a surprise."

I voice the last word loudly, and they come into the room, not running like I thought, but they are almost sheepishly entering, like they may have heard Mrs. Stratton's carnage talk.

I keep my gaze on Court to gauge his reaction.

I wish I hadn't.

Mrs. Stratton knows that of which she speaks.

MYSTERY

"ARE YOU MAD, Daddy?" Bristol's voice has lost all the excitement it's had the past few hours.

She sees his eyes as well.

They are burning with anger.

Burning.

He smiles and it's so fake I want to wipe it off. "You girls are beautiful. That's a nice style. Like your friend next door. Phoebe, right?"

"Yes. We even went to her stylist." Darling walks to the counter and picks up one of the bags. "Here's my hair, Daddy. It's going to make a little girl with cancer be able to have some hair."

"Here's mine," Bristol adds, shoving her bag into his hands. "Mommy would like that we did this, wouldn't she?"

I can't read Court anymore. He's a mixture of anger, hurt, surprise, disbelief. Just like this morning.

Texting was a great idea. I just needed to text the right word.

I know now if I had texted the word cut, the answer would have been no. We might have been able to work on him for a couple of weeks and changed his mind, but this is an absolute disaster.

"Shelby is going to print off the forms from the computer and we're going to fill them out. Then she's going to take us to the post office. We're doing the whole thing by ourselves. Are you proud of us, Daddy?"

Court can't take his gaze off the girls. He keeps touching their hair. "I am very proud of you girls. Now I need to talk to Shelby for a few minutes, so why don't you go back and watch a movie."

He places the bags of hair on the counter and stands to give them a hug. "Actually, it's kind of late. Get ready for bed, find a movie, and I'll be back in a little while to tuck you in."

"Okay." They hug Court before coming over to hug me. Their eyes search mine, like they know something isn't quite right. I give them a huge smile. "You girls look simply fabulous with your new hair. See you tomorrow."

Court nods to the living room as the girls walk down the hall to their bedrooms. I follow Court, unsure of everything I've been sure of these last few days.

Once again, everything has changed, only this time it's not for the better.

When we reach the living room, he turns. "You had no right," he says, shaking his head, "to do that."

"I texted. The wrong word, but I texted. Auto-correct is not my friend today." I smile, try to laugh, but the situation doesn't lend itself to anything humorous.

"Buying hair for kids with cancer is one thing. Cutting their hair off is another."

I reach out to touch him, but he backs up. My heart lurches, and I find it hard to swallow. Something is very off here. "Look. This is a mix-up. A bad one, but a mix-up nonetheless. Their hair will grow back. Fast probably."

"It's not about the hair."

He voices the words I was afraid to think.

"I know."

"With everything that happened today, everything that has been happening, the one constant I had was knowing the girls were their mother's daughters. They look like her. Act like her. As the days go by, it seems like they are the only good thing that has come from me marrying MaryLeigh. Is it too much for me to want them to stay like they are for a little while?"

As he speaks, he continues to put even more distance between us, like his words aren't doing enough damage. My heart is breaking into a million pieces, each one reminding me of a strand of tangled hair that has become my life.

I tried to fix it, but it's not mine to fix. "I've apologized. I can't uncut their hair. I can only tell you that I love you, that I would never do anything to hurt you, and that it breaks my heart to know you aren't ready to love again."

"That's not true." He still doesn't move, staying across the room from me. "I am ready. There are just some aspects of my life I don't want to change for now."

"This is about MaryLeigh and how she influenced the girls. But their tangled hair can't replace what you've lost. I see now MaryLeigh wasn't who you thought she was. That is evident, especially after what we found out today. But I thought that maybe this could be the beginning of something new. Something for us. I see now you'd rather live in the past when it comes to some things."

I walk out of the room hoping he will follow me.

I make it all the way to my room, let myself in and shut the door. His footsteps start down the hall, but they pass by my room and turn into the girls' rooms.

Minutes later I hear him walk past my room.

I knew he would.

No matter how much faith I have in us, if he doesn't have any this thing will never work.

Court may have told me he loved me, but he's still in love with something else.

Not someone, but something.

The idea of the wife he thought he had married.

FIVE O'CLOCK COMES early and I put on my running clothes. I tighten my visor and make sure my shoelaces are tied tightly. I look around the room one more time making sure I have everything.

It takes two trips to haul my things to the end of the driveway because I don't want to wake anyone by dragging my luggage down the hall. The cab I called should be here any minute. I write a note for the girls and leave it on the counter along with a note to Mrs. Stratton with Phoebe's number. I tell her the girls can probably play over there part of the day until they can find another nanny.

I sit in the back of the cab as it drives away in the dark gray of the Florida morning, knowing that it's what I have to do. I don't want to leave.

But I must.

The mystery of who MaryLeigh was, or wasn't, will continue to haunt

Court until he decides to break free from the past.

I can't give my heart to a man who doesn't have room in his for anything more than a broken dream. I get that the broken dream lives there.

I'd like to squeeze in and help heal the scars it left behind.

But he won't let me.

So I'll go.

I hate leaving Team Twin without saying goodbye, but I promised we'd Skype soon.

Court? I didn't leave a note because I didn't leave him.

He left me.

MARRIED

AUGUST IS HOT in Georgia, and it's even hotter on the steps of the porch of the trailer that Mama and Daddy live in.

Oh, and I'm living here with them for another couple of weeks until my apartment is available again. Daddy still hasn't gotten over the fact that he'll never get that introduction to Cal Treyhune that Court promised him over the Fourth of July weekend.

Mama knew right away this was a matter of the heart and not a matter of a job.

She's always been cool like that. Mama hasn't been nosy, but she let me know if I ever needed to talk she'd be there to listen.

I haven't wanted to talk yet.

Barb also has no less than three jobs lined up for me that are available whenever I'm ready to work.

I haven't been ready to do that either.

It's a shame to admit I've been hashing out this Court thing over and over in my mind. Jared called me once, but I didn't take the call. He didn't leave a message and that was fine by me.

Court?

He hasn't called once. And it's been over three weeks.

Three weeks of misery for me.

But I think the worst of it is over.

I'm on the upswing now and am feeling okay.

Not fine or good, mind you, but just okay.

It's a step up from miserable and melancholy.

Some of the kids from the trailer park are running around playing tag. I like watching them. They remind me of the crazy days with Team Twin. I can finally think about them without tearing up. I'm going to Skype them soon, but I haven't had the guts to do so yet.

I also never finished that homeschooling project Court had me working on. I'm sure he's got all that figured out now.

At least Jared doesn't have to worry about me taking his job.

The kids start running again, but they are all running in the same direction. Toward the road.

Oh, there's a car coming.

Probably somebody they don't know. They're kind of scary when a stranger invades their space.

I should know. They surrounded my car the first few times I came in here. Now they're used to me.

Sometimes the younger ones wave.

Sometimes the older ones give me the finger.

Either way I smile and drive slowly to my parents' driveway.

This car is driving really slow and the kids are pointing excitedly. Must be a nice car.

As the car comes fully into view I realize it's not just a nice car, it's a limo. A big, black, sleek limo.

And it stops in front of my parents' trailer.

My heart starts to beat faster.

The driver gets out, walks to the door and opens it. A lady steps out, then a man.

I put my hand over my chest as I realize it's Court's parents.

His parents?

Cal and Vera Treyhune are here?

They walk up the short walkway to where I'm sitting. I run my hand down my plain pink T-shirt and push my hand through hair that I haven't washed in two days.

Or brushed for that matter. "Hi," I say.

"Hello there, young lady with the darn good name. Shelby. It's good to see you."

Cal looks good. He looks like the guy I have seen on the television screen. Strong, commanding. A far cry from the man I saw in North Carolina on Father's Day.

I want to scream "why are you here?" But I don't. I try to stay calm and keep it cool. Like it's the most natural thing in the world for them to show up at my parents' trailer on any given day. "It's good to see you, too."

"Hi, honey," Vera says.

"Hi." I wave at her, now becoming nervous at their visit. Is something wrong? Are the twins okay?

Cal clears his throat. "Vera and I have come for two reasons. First, Court told me he promised your papa that we'd meet someday. Well, today's the day. Is he home?"

"Yes, sir, he is. Let me get him." I start up the stairs, then hit my forehead with my hand. I turn back and face Cal and Vera. "I'm sorry. How rude. Would you like to come in?"

Cal smiles. "That will be fine."

My hand shakes slightly as I pull the screen door open. "Daddy, there's somebody here to see you."

I don't even know how we made it through the next hour. I thought Mama was going to shoot me for inviting strangers in, and then Dad about fell out, literally back into his chair, when he realized it was Cal Treyhune that had interrupted his episode of Dr. Phil.

Dr. Phil was forgotten immediately and replaced with conversation that didn't stop until Mama asked anyone if they wanted a drink. After glasses of sweet tea were poured and given out, the conversation resumed again like everyone was old friends.

Finally there is a lull in the conversation and Cal looks at me. "Shelby, girl. I told you earlier we came here for two reasons. Do you want to know what the second reason is?"

"That would be nice. You've had me on the edge of my seat for the past hour," I joke.

Half joke.

I've been sitting here for the last hour trying to figure out the other reason he and Vera showed up here in a limo at my parents' trailer.

A trailer much like the one they started out in, they told my parents.

Cal waves his hand toward the door. "Go on out to the limo and look in the back seat."

"Right now?"

"No, tomorrow. Of course right now. Scoot. We'll wait here."

I set my glass of tea down and walk out the door, still barefoot, still wearing my cutoffs and my plain tee.

The closer I get to the limo, the more nervous I become.

Is it a present from the girls?

From Court?

As I approach the big, black, shiny limo, the driver steps out. His expression doesn't give anything away. He simply walks to the door and places his hand on the handle, like he's waiting for me to approach before he opens it.

The limo is so quiet I barely notice it's still running. When the driver opens the door, a blast of cool air hits me.

"You can get in, miss. I think someone is expecting you."

More confused than ever, and grateful for the cool air, I climb into the limo. At first I don't see anything, but I do smell Court's clean scent.

And then I see him.

Sitting on the side seat, smiling.

I slink into the back seat not believing he's been sitting out here for over an hour.

"Hi."

With one word he has my heart missing him all over again.

"Hi." I swallow hard wondering how his heart feels.

"I've missed you."

His words fall on me like they can change things. But they can't. Simply missing someone isn't enough to make a life together. Do I dare admit that I've missed him? Just like his words can't change anything, mine can't either. "I've missed you, too."

I watch his reaction to my words but am unprepared for the magnitude of his smile. His smile makes my heart flip at the possibilities of why he is here.

Why he seems so happy and carefree.

Carefree?

Set free?

I refuse to think he's here for any other reason than chaperoning his parents. Because if I do, my slightly put-back-together heart might break into more tiny pieces. Pieces so tiny they can never possibly be reconstructed.

"You were right, you know."

His voice is smooth. Unassuming. Confident. "I was?"

He sits straighter in the seat, his head almost touching the top of the limo. His fingertips steeple together, tapping each other. "You were. I was hanging onto something that I had envisioned for so long that I couldn't believe not only that it was over, but that it had never really existed to begin with."

"Court, I'm sorry—"

He holds his hand up. "You have nothing to be sorry for. I'm the one who's sorry. I'm sorry it took me so long to see what I had right in front of me. I couldn't see past that tangled mess the girls' hair had become, just like my life, and then when it was gone, I was scared."

"Scared?"

"Everything had changed. For the better, I know, but I was still afraid to take a chance on you and me. Still afraid to believe in someone, not something."

Was still afraid. Was? In the past? "And now?"

"Now I see what I let walk out of my door. I should have known that morning when you were gone and I was devastated that I needed to call you, see you, explain. But no. I was going to let you leave if that's what you wanted."

A heaviness settles on my heart as I hear his confession. His explanation at letting me go. I guess he came to ease his conscious. "I'm glad you've figured some things out. Maybe you can move forward now. With life."

I want to say with love, but since that won't be with me I'm not encouraging that direction. There's only so much a girl can take.

"Have you fallen out of love with me?"

My face flushes while I try to keep my breathing at a steady pace. Would he ask if he didn't care? Would he ask if he didn't want to know the truth?

He's lived for a while avoiding the truth.

He can't avoid it forever.

Only the truth is good enough for a moment like this. "There's not enough depth in the world for me to fall that far."

His Adam apple swallows like he's fighting emotion.

Within moments he's next to me. His gaze locks onto mine, and I can't look away.

I don't want to look away.

My fingers brush the soft, dark hair at his temple, the need to make sure he's real overwhelming me.

I wonder at the absurdity of it all. The slow torture I'm putting myself through. Seeing him again is like nothing I expected. Aloof and simply friendship can never be in our picture.

It's either all or nothing for me.

I pray he knows this.

"Shelby, I love you. I have no idea of what lies ahead, but I can promise you one thing. For the first time I have faith that this is right. Faith that you'll be mine forever. Come back to Florida. Will you?"

My eyes moisten, and I don't care if he sees my tears. "Yes. And I am yours forever."

His arms wrap around me and his lips descend on mine, reminding me of one of the reasons I love him so.

His kiss also brings me to a place that's so much like home. Where I know I belong.

And that place has nothing to do with limos and luxury.

It has everything to do with faith and the heart.

My heart, his heart.

Together forever.

"I love you so much," I say between kisses.

The door to the limo opens, bringing in a blast of hot, Georgia air.

Court and I can't untangle ourselves quickly enough to keep Team Twin from witnessing our kissing festival.

"Shelby!" Bristol climbs into the limo, Darling right behind her, and they scramble to the seat Court vacated.

A circle of completeness surrounds the atmosphere. Court's arm is still touching mine, and two beautiful girls with amazingly cute hair are staring at me.

"Where did you come from?" I ask, hoping to deter any questions about why I am sitting so close to their father.

"When it became apparent you were going to be awhile, I let them go and play with the kids." He turns his attention to the girls. "Did you guys have fun?"

"We did." Bristol now eyes him with suspicion. "Why were you kissing Shelby?"

"Why do you think?" Court asks.

"Because you're getting married?" Darling asks.

"Wow," I say. "I think that's jumping the gun a little."

"I think it's a perfect idea." Court grabs my left hand. "Yes, a nice shiny diamond will look great right there." He points to my ring finger.

I look at the man I love, then turn my attention to the girls that have given me a lot of grief, but also a lot of joy. The joy is worth it.

Turning back to Court I ask, "Have I just become engaged?"

He rubs my ring finger with his thumb. "You have. Ring to follow. Big ring."

Sitting in a limo in the trailer park of my parents' home is the last place I ever pictured becoming engaged. Yes, I am on the outskirts of nowhere important, but somebody important has my heart in his. "I don't need a big ring. I need you."

He brushes a kiss across my ring finger. "You have me. Forever, remember?"

"I remember." I hug Court, my head resting on his shoulder, my gaze drifting out of the door Team Twin left open. My parents' home is in full view.

Yes, home.

With Court's help I finally see how rich my parents have always been.

And now I can be just as rich in my own life.

Standing in faith.

With the man I love.

THE END

DISCUSSION QUESTIONS

1. Shelby is ashamed of her childhood. Have you ever felt that way? If so, why?
2. Shelby has an unrealistic view of what the word successful means. How do you define success? Would you be willing to act like someone you aren't to give the impression you are successful?
3. Bristol and Darling prove to be a hand full for Shelby. Have you ever had a job that you were unprepared for?
4. Shelby took a job in another state trying to distance herself from her former fiancé. Have you ever tried to physically distance yourself from a bad situation?
5. Do you think Court was hiding behind his work because of Paula's death or deception?
6. Even though Court denies he has faith in anything he shows a lot of faith in his best friend Jared for a long time. Have you ever stood by someone even though they may have not done the right things all the time?
7. Have you ever surprised someone like Shelby was able to surprise her father? How did that person react?
8. How long would you have let Bristol and Darling go without brushing their hair?
9. Did you like Jared? Why or why not?
10. What was your favorite scene and why?

Dear Reader,

I've had so much fun writing about Hampton Cove. Thank you to everyone who has read these stories. They are a work of fiction, yet their messages are from the heart. Things don't make us rich.

Who we are in Jesus Christ makes our lives rich..

I thank my husband in every book and will continue to do so. His support is amazing. I literally couldn't do this without him.

Thank you to Emily Sewell for editing.

Thank you to Missy Tippens. Your insight into my stories always makes them better. Ciara Knight. What can I say? This girl not only rocks critiquing, but you wouldn't be reading this if it wasn't for her. Seriously, she has taught me so much, and what I struggle with she graciously offers to do.

Georgia Romance Writers, ACFW, and New Life Writers. Thank for great teachings and support.

My family is always supporting and amazing. Brenna, Chris, Caleb, Alex, Sarah, Melanie, Jason, Ally B, Tyler, Lisa and Brian. You are my life!

Jesus Christ—my savior, my strength, my sustainer, my all in all. You give me love and hope and life.

ABOUT THE AUTHOR

Award winning and USA Today featured author Lindi Peterson lives in the foothills of the Blue Ridge Mountains with her husband, 1 dog, 3 cats and 3 birds. Lindi loves sharing life with her family and friends. Her passion for reading led her to writing. When God spoke words of love into her heart her life was forever changed. You can find Lindi at:

Lindipeterson.com
@lindipeterson
Thefaithgirls.com
Inspyromance.com

www.ingramcontent.com/pod-product-compliance
Lightning Source LLC
Chambersburg PA
CBHW031952170626
46807CB00006B/2460